D1573030

Sleepless

Michael Omer

For Liora

Author's Note

This book is about a town called Narrowdale. This is not a real town, and will not be found on any map.
Which is probably a good thing.
There are several links in this book. These links are actual live links to Amy's blog. Though they are not crucial for the story, Amy is awesome and her blog is fun to read.
Amy is also fictional, as are the rest of the characters in this book.

CHAPTER ONE

"Sweetie, we're here," Mom announces. I shut my eyes, listening to the sounds that set a new chapter of my life into motion. The engine dies; Mom's seatbelt unbuckles; her car door opens, then closes.

"Amy. Amy? Let's go, we're here. I need your help with the luggage."

My eyes open for lack of any other option. Mom is already huffing by the trunk, hauling out bags and suitcases. She is inexplicably brimming with energy. I slowly push the passenger's door open and get out of the car. The sun is scorching, punishing us with California's August heat. The air stands completely still, not even a trace of wind. Mom hands me a duffel bag full of clothes.

I stare at the row of identical houses in front of me. Each house has a small front lawn, a wooden fence, and unremarkable white walls. The same six windows face the street from each house, and the same brown front door is positioned in the same place. Some residents have tried to create a unique atmosphere by hanging tasteless decorations on the doors, or by positioning flower pots in strategic places. However, their efforts only emphasize the futility of their struggle. The whole street emanates a drab, cheerless feeling. Ugh.

"Where's the house?" I ask.

"That one right there, sweetie." Mom points at one of the house clones. "Number thirteen."

"How do you know it's the right one?"

"That's easy. It's number thirteen. The others have a different number." She looks at me, grinning. I'm not sure if she's making fun of me. Mom has an odd sense of humor sometimes.

"Remind me once more, what exactly are we doing here?"

Mom shuts her eyes and does that breathing thing that she sometimes does. I can almost hear her counting to ten. She then opens her eyes and looks at me. "Amy, we have a lot of work, and the cable guy is about to arrive in ten minutes. Let's get to it, okay?"

"Okay." I shrug. "Do you have the key?"

Mom rummages in her purse, cries in dismay, and rummages some more. I've seen this happen before. Mom's purse conceals secret worlds and dimensions within it. To find something in there usually requires a search party. I already know what is going to happen. Sure enough, after a few seconds of hysterical searching, she walks to the front of the car and empties the purse on the hood. Among the different papers, cosmetics, packs of chewing gums and various other objects, a single key shines in the sunlight.

"There it is." She sighs in relief. She stuffs the purse's contents back into it and walks with me to the uninviting brown door of our new home. She unlocks it. "Welcome to Thirteen Maple Street."

"Why was the house locked, anyway? Are you worried that someone might steal the floor tiles?" I step inside the empty house. My words echo around the empty room unpleasantly. The front door opens to an open space. The kitchen, to my right, is almost completely bare. It has a refrigerator, a sink, and some presumably empty cupboards. The room to my left is probably the living room, though I can't be entirely sure. Where will everything go? It all seems so… small.

"You might find it strange, but people sometimes steal faucets," Mom says, dropping a suitcase on the floor. "That's why the house was locked."

"It looks a bit small," I say, earning the understatement of the month award.

"It will look larger once it has some furniture in it," Mom answers.

"That makes no sense at all."

Mom ignores me, checking the kitchen. "I don't like the way they installed the sink," she mutters.

"It's a sink. What's not to like?" I ask. She ignores me some more.

I look around. There are several closed doors. Which one hides my room behind it?

"Mom, where's my room?"

"It's upstairs, sweetie. First door to the left."

I run up the stairs to the second floor. There are four doors. All bedrooms? I open the first door to the left. Okay, it's a room. A small room. Why is everything so small? The walls are completely bare, freshly painted. Mom and Dad bought this house when it was still being built, and we're the first to live in it. One of the walls has a big window with a view of... well, of nothing, actually, just a boring street. But a window is nice. In LA my window was smaller. There, Amy, think positive. Not everything is small. The window is big. Yippee.

I check out the other rooms. There is another one which is almost the same as mine. I assume this will be Anthony's. Another door opens to the bathroom. The last door opens to a larger room with its own separate bathroom. Mom and Dad's, probably.

I walk back to Anthony's room. The most important thing now is to make sure mine is better than his. Actually, they are completely identical. Same size, same window, same walls... I look out of Anthony's window. Its view is partly blocked by the adjacent house. Ha! I win. I descend the stairs feeling a bit more pleased.

I start exploring the bottom floor, but the humidity and the stuffiness drain my energy. My eyes roam around, searching for the air conditioning. Ah! There we go. I approach it and turn it on. Nothing happens.

"Mom! How do I turn on the air conditioning?"

"Just press the button, sweetie."

"I pressed it."

"Amy, I'm really busy. Can't we handle this later?"

"Later? I might not survive until later! You could boil an egg in this house just by putting it on the floor. It's so hot I could–"

"All right, all right," she snaps and joins me. She presses the same button that I pressed. Nothing happens.

"Your father probably knows how to activate it," she says.

"It isn't rocket science. It's an air conditioner."

"Then why don't you figure it out?" She sounds highly irritated.

Fine. I press some smaller buttons. I turn a dial. I thump it lightly. Nothing. I simply can't believe this. We're stuck with no air conditioning until Dad gets here! In August! What could be worse?

"Don't bother helping me, sweetie, I'm doing fine on my own," Mom says behind me.

Mom has countless ways of saying "sweetie." There's "Well done, sweetie!" when I tell her about an exam I scored high on. There's the sweetie of "Sweetie, can you please pass the salt?" That's the sweetie that comes with a polite request. There's the frequent sweetie of "I'm going out, sweetie," just an ordinary sweetie, punctuating her sentences. The sweetie I just got, "Don't bother, sweetie," is a sweetie brimming with implications. Rivers of frustration and annoyance lurk behind this sweetie. When this sweetie shows its vicious head, one should be careful.

I promptly walk outside and help Mom haul the rest of the luggage inside. I take my laptop and put it with the rest of my bags. Once the movers arrive with my table, I'll take it to my room. Unfortunately, getting the luggage inside was completely meaningless, since we can't unpack yet. Dad hasn't arrived with the movers, and there are no closets in the rooms. I'm not even sure why our clothes had to ride with me and Mom, and not with the moving truck. It's one of Mom's strange quirks.

A knock on the door. It's the cable guy. He asks if by any chance we have some coffee. We have no coffee, no pot, and no mugs. He shrugs and asks Mom where we intend to put the TV.

"Never mind that," I say quickly. "Can you figure out how to turn on the air conditioning?"

He walks over to the unit and presses the same button. Naturally, nothing happens.

"Huh," he says. "It doesn't seem to work. Pity, it's hot in here."

"My husband will be here shortly. He knows how to turn on the air conditioning," Mom says, looking at me sharply. "We are going to put one television in the living room, and another one upstairs, let me show you where."

They walk upstairs, and I am left downstairs with nothing to do. Out of habit, I pull out my phone, and then immediately put it back in my pocket. I don't want to call my friends, living their wonderful life in LA in their wonderfully air conditioned homes. When Mom and Dad told me that we were moving, I was completely devastated. I loved LA! I loved my home, loved my neighborhood, loved my life. There wasn't even a good explanation for the sudden relocation. Mom said that they wanted a house to call their own, that they didn't want to rent anymore, that we'd have a nice back yard. When I argued that there was nothing wrong with renting and that I didn't care about back yards, they just told me that this was their decision, and that I should get used to the idea.

Yeah, well, it would be easier to get used to the idea if it were a bit cooler.

I wander aimlessly around the ground floor. I open a door, encountering a toilet and a sink. They're both shiny and clean, completely unused. I close the door and open a different one. An empty room. Several paint stains tarnish the floor. This room, like all the other rooms in the house, is painted white. Through the window in the opposite wall, I can see the neighbor's front yard. Apparently, the neighbor likes grass. It's the only thing growing in his yard. Just a big patch of lawn, with no trees or flowers to break the monotony. I walk back to the house's entrance and notice another door, yet unexplored. I open it.

Darkness. Suffocation. Something in this complete blackout makes me nervous, and my hand fumbles for the light switch. Where is it? Why can't I find it? Even though I'm standing in the doorway, the darkness envelops me completely, blocking out the light behind me, and I feel trapped, helpless. Deep within the room's vast space I can hear water dripping. I decide to get out, close the door behind me, but... where is the door? I whirl around, panicking. I try to feel around for the door's handle...

The light suddenly turns on. My mom is standing next to me. We are both inside a small, windowless room.

"This is the storage room, sweetie," Mom says. "The light switch is just here, by the door."

"Oh… Okay," I say, my heart still pounding. "I think we have a leak here. I heard dripping."

We both become silent, listening. I strain my ears, hearing nothing. Mom walks in, trying to spot a leak in the wall, a puddle, anything.

"I can't see a leak," Mom says. "But I'll ask Dad to check it out."

"Excuse me?" the cable guy calls from the other room. "Can you please show me the exact location where you want to put the TV?"

Mom leaves me and walks away to talk to him. I quickly follow her, taking deep breaths. Unbelievable. I feel like a baby, afraid of the dark. But something happened in there. For a moment I was trapped, I was lost. And I felt… I almost felt as if there was something or someone threatening nearby. I shiver, despite the heat. Stupid. I scared myself silly.

Feeling a need to distance myself from the storage room, I walk outside and look around. The street is completely deserted. It's noon. No one goes outside in the middle of the day in August. Well, almost no one.

A middle-aged man is standing in the doorway of the adjacent house, watching me. He's almost entirely bald, the last strands of black hair decorating the edges of his head. He is dressed in a button-down square-patterned shirt and old wrinkled jeans which have seen better days. Next to him sits a huge white dog, its tongue lolling, observing me as well. Their stares make me uncomfortable.

"Hello," I say.

He looks at me. "Hello. Are you the new neighbors?"

"Yes. We're moving in today," I say. He looks at me expectantly. What does he want? "My name is Amy," I add.

"Nice to meet you." He nods again. I wait patiently for him to introduce himself, but this doesn't seem to be forthcoming.

"What's your name?" I finally ask.

"I'm Alex," he answers. "And you?"

"Me?" I gawk at him in confusion. "I'm Amy. I just said… Yes. Amy."

"Have a nice day," he says and enters his home, the dog following him.

Weird guy. This place sucks. What was wrong with LA? Why did we need to move to Narrowdale? We had such a nice apartment, with nice neighbors. Narrowdale. What kind of place is this, anyway? Who's even heard of Narrowdale? I don't want to live here, I want…

I can hear a large engine roaring. Looking down the street, I spot a truck driving towards me. I stare at it until it grinds to a halt next to our new home. The passenger's door opens and Dad gets out.

"Hi, Amy, we're here." He smiles. "Let's move away from the entrance. We're in the movers' path."

I move away from the entrance. I wish I could move a lot more. Move back to LA.

CHAPTER TWO

The movers have already brought my dresser, bed, wardrobe and desk to my room. The familiar furniture improves my mood significantly. I just wish it wasn't so hot. My shirt is sticking to my back unpleasantly. My hair feels all messed up from the humidity. My legs keep itching under my pants. Aaaaargh!

"Dad!" I yell.

Nothing. I walk around the house and find him in the bedroom, unpacking bed sheets.

"Dad!" I say. "Can you please fix the air conditioning? I'm dying here!"

"Oh, I tried," he says. "Looks like it's broken."

I stare at him blankly. "But… it's new," I stammer.

"It is," he agrees. "but we forgot to check it before we moved. I already called the air conditioning guy. He apologized and promised he'll come over next week."

"He apologized?" I am fuming.

"Yes."

"He… do you know what this means… I… next week?" I am in complete overload. "We need to sue him! He should go to prison!"

"That might be a bit harsh," Dad says. "It was a simple mistake."

"A simple mistake? He's the air conditioning guy! He had just one job! Doesn't he take pride in his work?"

"Amy, don't you have some unpacking to do?"

I walk back to my room, furious. Next week. I take off my shoes and socks. The socks are soggy with sweat. Disgusting. I can't believe I have to carry on like this until next week!

I empty two bags full of clothes on my bed. Most of them I refold, wondering how I should organize my wardrobe. Usually my everyday shirts go on the second shelf, and the pants below. But the closet is completely empty; this is a great chance to reorganize. Yes! Carpe diem! Shirts down, pants up! It's time to shake things up, to really go wild!

No, on second thought, this is no good at all. The shirts go back to the top shelf.

When I am done with folding my underwear, putting them in their drawer, I'm completely soaked in sweat. I decide to take my first shower in my new home. First of all I find the box with the shampoo and the soap. I open it impatiently, tearing off the top. I had the foresight to pack some towels in the same box as well. Well done, Amy. Where is the laundry basket? A real mystery. I should ask Mom. I drop my dirty clothes in the corner of the bathroom. The sensation of cold water on my body is amazing. If only I could live in here! But obviously, I can't. I turn off the water, wrap myself with the towel and walk back to my room.

As I am looking through my clothes for a more fitting outfit for this heat, my phone rings. It's Nicole.

"Honey!!!" Nicole screams into my ear. "How is the new place?"

"Hot," I report. "The air conditioner isn't working."

"What do you mean?"

"Apparently the guy who installed the air conditioning failed to… you know, actually install it so that it works. Guess when he's coming to finish the job? Next week."

A long conversation ensues, regarding people who should be ashamed of themselves. Nicole suggests I come back to LA and sleep at her place until school starts. Thanks, but really, I have to arrange my closet, and I guess I have to help Mom set up the house. I am having a hard time dressing with one hand as Nicole yammers on. Yeah, my room is cute, I'll send pictures. Yes, I will update the blog. Bye.

Where are the bed sheets? I think I saw them in one of the boxes in the living room. I leave the room to search for them, and Mom catches me.

"Amy, can you please take the box with Grandma's plates to the storage room?"

The storage room. My heart sinks. "Why? Why not unpack them in the kitchen?"

"Because we never use them," Mom says, giving me a meaningful look. Her look is meant to convey the words 'They have that hideous rose pattern, and we all believe they are uglier than garden slugs.'

"Then why don't we throw them away?"

"Because they were Grandma's, and they were very expensive."

"Then why–"

"Amy, I am really busy. Just do it, please."

I lift the box unhappily. Through a crack in the box's lid I can see one of the plates and it is indeed a plate which deserves to be stored in a storage room. I approach the door and stop for a moment, considering asking Mom to open the door for me as my hands are full… eventually I decide to handle this on my own. I'm really not afraid of a dark room. I lay my hand on the doorknob, and for a moment I can almost hear dripping water again. I fling the door wide open…

It's just a storage room. Grandma's plates go in. They'll come out when she comes over to visit.

Mom spots me closing the door. "Good. Now please unpack the rest of the plates in the kitchen."

I groan and start unpacking. Within a minute I am sweating again. Yuck.

Once Mom disappears somewhere, I sneak back into the shower. Where's the laundry basket? I really should ask Mom. Additional dirty clothes pile on the previous ones. I leave the shower refreshed and peek into the living room. Mom's not there. I locate two boxes, one with my sheets, the other with books, posters, and my desk lamp; in short, all the stuff that makes me feel at home. I take them one at a time to my room and unpack them happily. My phone rings again. It's Jennifer Williams.

"What's up, Jennifer?"

"Still alive," she answers in a morose tone. "And you? How's the house?"

"Hot. The air conditioner doesn't work. The air conditioner guy messed up."

Yes, it's unbelievable that people actually get paid to do nothing. We talk on while I lie down on my bed to rest a little. Jennifer suggests drinking a lot of cold water, and taking numerous showers. Thanks, I say, for these wonderful, original ideas. The room is very cute. I'll update the blog. Bye!

Where did I put my laptop? A moment of pure panic... Oh, right, I left it in the living room. Where all the movers are hanging around. What was I thinking? I run hysterically downstairs, my heart thumping. If it's gone... It's not gone. There it is, exactly where I put it. The movers are nice guys. They wouldn't steal from a fourteen-year-old girl.

I pick the laptop up... and Mom walks into the living room.

"There you are!" says the predator gleefully as it catches its helpless prey. "I need some assistance. Can you please unpack Anthony's things in his room?"

"Why can't Anthony unpack Anthony's things?" I grumble.

"Because Anthony is at college, and he's not coming over until Friday," she answers impatiently.

"Yeah, so he can unpack his stuff then! It's no big deal..."

"Amy! We don't see Anthony a lot, and I want him to feel really at home when he comes here. Can you please do this one thing that I ask?" She gives me a look as if the weight of the world is resting on her shoulders.

An A score for the guilt trip, Mom. You didn't ask for only one thing today. This is like... the hundredth thing. But fine, whatever. I sigh and take the bag with Anthony's clothes up to his room. Mom and Dad are always so frantic before Anthony comes over. Anthony has to feel welcome. Anthony has to feel comfortable. We should cook whatever Anthony wants to eat. It's like having royalty over for the weekend, except this specific member of the royal family sleeps all the time, sits in his boxer shorts in the living room, and does almost nothing except watch TV.

I get my revenge on him in a typical and mature way. I open the bag with his clothes and start unpacking imaginatively. The shirts are placed on a shelf accessible only if he gets a ladder. I hide all of his socks within a mountain of pants, and the clothes which should be hung up I crumple into a big ball and shove in a corner. The underwear I sprinkle all around the closet, just like small flakes of underwear snow. No one can say I don't do as I'm told. I've unpacked his clothes.

Oh, this heat… For god's sake! A week? I won't survive two days! Straight to the shower.

The dirty clothes find their way to the pile. It's a little mountain. A miniature model of Everest, made out of dirty laundry. The… Launderest? I should really talk to Mom about the thing with the basket. Oh well. Flowing water, feels nice. I can dimly hear my phone ring from my room. Never mind, I'll call back later. One second, two seconds, three… There's really no reason to leave the shower in a rush… Four, five… Perhaps it's important? Six, seven… It must be urgent, they're not letting up! I turn the water off, wrap myself in a towel, run out of the bathroom… Eight, nine… My feet are wet, I slip and fall down, hurt my knee… Ten, eleven… I answer the phone.

"What happened?" I ask, panting.

"Amy! How is the new home?" It's Jennifer Scott.

"Oh, wonderful."

"Yeah? Everything's fine?"

"Yup. Splendid. No complaints at all. It's very nice here."

"That's so great!"

"Sure. Greater than life."

That's right, Narrowdale is a terrific place. It's really pleasant. I can hardly feel the heat. Crying? Of course not, I just hurt my knee, no big deal. Yes, I'll update the blog.

"Amy." Mom enters the room and looks at me. "Is everything okay?"

"Yes, I just hurt my knee."

"Right. Did you see the laundry basket?"

"The laundry…"

"Oh, there it is. What's it doing in your room?" She moves the bags, revealing the basket.

"I don't know."

"Maybe you should rest a little, sweetie, you're working really hard."

"Yes Mom."

"And drink a lot of cold water. It's really hot in here."

"Yes. Hot."

"Next week the air conditioning guy is coming."

"Good."

"You've organized your room really nicely."

"Thanks."

She closes the door.

I wipe my tears, put some clothes on and turn on my laptop. I bet I don't have Internet access… There's Internet! Praise God! Thank you, wonderful cable guy, I'm connected to the world!

I type in the link to my blog:

http://amy.strangerealm.com/newplace.html

CHAPTER THREE

By Friday, I already feel like I want to kill everyone. The heat is making all of us cranky; I am not the only one complaining. I overheard Mom screaming at the air conditioning guy over the phone, warning him that the air conditioning better be fixed by the beginning of next week, or there would be consequences. I don't know what these consequences are. When Mom says something like that to me, this usually means that I'm grounded. I can't really see her doing that to the air conditioning guy.

Additionally, all the cleaning, unpacking and organizing of the house is driving me insane. There are some clothes that I simply can't find. I'm sure I packed them, but somehow during the move they disappeared into the realm of lost clothes. I have four different socks which are completely alone, their companions lost forever. One of those socks is a member of my favorite pair. I spent forty-five minutes going through all of my stuff, looking for the other sock, with no luck. It must be sad, being a sock with no twin.

Finally, on Friday morning, I decide that anything is better than spending another minute in this hot, suffocating, chaotic environment. I find a second when Mom is not around and notify Dad that I'm going to the mall. My Dad, knowing that women sometimes have to go to malls, says okay, and before he has second thoughts, I disappear from his sight.

Astonishingly, the heat outside is not as bad as inside the house. It's terrible, absolutely, but I have learned that there is a scale of terribleness and the heat outside is merely a… let's say seven.

The mall is a twenty-minute walk from my home, and I actually enjoy the fresh air and the sunlight. Slowly, I feel like I can be around human beings again without wishing to stab them repeatedly with a breadknife. It's nice.

This is also my first opportunity to observe Narrowdale on my own, and not through the car window.

It's... boring.

Narrowdale is essentially a suburban town, just an hour and a half driving distance from LA. The residents seem to think that there is nothing finer than having a small house with a small backyard to live in. The parks all exist for the sole intention of supplying moms with a way to pass the time with their small children during the afternoon. The streets are clean and nearly empty, probably due to the heat. Obviously, other people do not have problems with their air conditioning units. There is almost no traffic, and a slight feeling of drowsiness is felt all around. After living in LA for my entire life, it feels almost as if someone pressed the mute button all over the town.

The mall, once I reach it, offers mainly disappointments. The building itself is drab and unwelcoming. There is one café, named, rather unimaginatively, "Alfred's." The stores are all small businesses with old supplies, old carpets and old customers.

With little hope I enter the only clothing store which seems to be aimed at people my age. My sliver of hope quickly disintegrates as I walk through the shop spotting knock offs of clothes which were fashionable three years ago. The man at the counter is having an argument with a middle-aged woman.

"I am telling you, the shirt is no good!" the woman says angrily. "I would like a full refund!"

"As I've already said, our refund policy is one month, and the shirt has to be in good condition," the man answers patiently.

"But it's your fault that the shirt is torn." The woman stamps her foot. "You promised that it would keep the cats at bay. You promised! The cats are the ones who scratched it!"

This last sentence draws my attention. I've heard many discussions about clothes, but usually cats aren't included in them. Unless it's cat hair.

"Look." The woman holds up the shirt. "This scratch – from the grey cat across the street. This one from the ginger cat, the one I told you about. This part is fine, but there was a small black cat which bit me through it. This shirt clearly didn't do its job!"

"Well, did you–" the man behind the counter suddenly notices me and becomes quiet. The woman sees his stare and also quiets down. They both stare at me.

"Can I help you?" the man asks.

"Um... Just looking around," I say.

"Okay," he says. His tone does not sound as if it is okay. He actually sounds as if that is the worst thing that could happen, a customer walking in and looking at clothes. I decide to leave. As I am leaving I hear the woman whispering to him "And they also scratched my legs! It's entirely your fault!"

Weird. So far, Narrowdale's residents do not impress me. That woman was crazy! Why wasn't she kicked out of the store? It almost seemed as if the man behind the counter was having a discussion with her – a woman who is clearly out of her mind! I walk out shaking my head. This mall is ridiculous. It would fit inside some of the smaller malls in LA. There's absolutely nothing here. Except... My eye catches the tiny ice cream shop.

I have thirty-five dollars so I can easily buy a comforting chocolate shake. I immerse myself in the image of the cold shake slowly drawn into my mouth through a straw...

"Excuse me, do you have any money?"

The man who just addressed me looks appalling. He's dressed in an old, square-patterned shirt that used to be white, though now it is several shades of brown and gray. His pants, brown and torn, are huge and on the verge of falling down, and the only thing holding them up is a fraying old belt. He has no shoes, only socks; both of them have holes through which dirty toes protrude. His bearded face is covered in all kinds of dirt and grime. An awful stench emanates from him, and I find myself holding my breath. In LA people like this would sometimes hang around in the parks and streets, but here? In Narrowdale? In a mall?

"I don't have any money," I quickly say, taking a step back.

He looks hurt. "Not polite to lie. You have thirty-five dollars in your bag. Just say you don't feel like giving any of them to me."

What? How did he know how much money I had? "No. really, I have no–" Another step back.

"Thirty-five dollars. I understand. You're hungry and hot. You want that chocolate shake. You have no good reason to give me your money. After all, Edgar's just some guy living on the street. But you know what? I never lie."

I am breathing in short, hurried breaths, and there is a bitter taste in my mouth. I've encountered homeless people before. Some of them have talked to me, and two even tried to touch me, but this man somehow frightens me much more. What the hell is going on here? How did he know...

"I know a lot of things. I know what the trees whisper to each other. I know the sad woman that no one sees, walking around here every night. I know of your friend and the moon..." He squints. "Why does he like the moon so much?"

"Edgar, leave the girl alone."

Edgar turns and grins at the speaker. He is tall, dressed in a blue uniform, which fits him tightly. His face is calm, and his eyes are watching us both with a serious expression. I look at him pleadingly. Help me, rescue me.

"What's up, Edgar? Why are you harassing little girls?"

Little girls? What little girls?

"I am not harassing any little girls," says Edgar, looking confused. "I am just talking to the lady here. She doesn't realize where she is. She has no idea what happens in Narrowdale."

"Edgar," the guy says with a sigh. "Did you eat today?"

"Just a small breakfast."

"Okay." He pulls a wallet from his pocket and draws out a five-dollar bill. "Here. Go get yourself something to eat. But only food, all right? Nothing else."

Edgar takes the money and smiles. "Peter, do you want to know–"

"I don't want to know anything. Go on. Enjoy your meal."

Edgar winks at me and shuffles away towards the back of the mall.

"He really is harmless," says the guy in the uniform. "He's just a bit confused. He never hurts anyone."

I nod.

"Are you all right? You're shaking a bit."

"Yeah, I mean… He just scared me a little." I try to relax, taking a deep breath. "He said… He knew… " I realize that trying to explain what just happened would make me sound crazy. "It's nothing. He just surprised me."

"Are you on your way home? Where do you live?"

"Close by, on Maple Street."

"Okay, I'm walking in the same direction. I'll walk you home."

I consider refusing. I don't know this guy, but if Edgar comes back… "Thanks."

"My name is Peter."

I look at Peter. He's about eighteen, maybe nineteen. He's tall, with strong, wide shoulders. He has a crew cut, and a cute half smile. His eyes are big, dark brown; they seem soft and warm. I suddenly realize that he's introduced himself and I haven't said anything for a couple of seconds. I blush and say, "Amy. I mean that's my name. Amy. Are you a cop?"

"No, I work for a security firm." He smiles at me.

"What do you secure?" We start walking.

"Narrowdale. My firm got the contract to make sure Narrowdale's secure. Two roadblocks, one perimeter patrol."

I keep silent, trying to understand. Why on earth would a half-asleep town like Narrowdale need any security, let alone roadblocks and perimeter patrols?

"There are a few of us and we take shifts," he tries to clarify. "For my shift I patrol around the town, making sure that all is well."

"And what if all is not well?"

"Usually, all is well."

"This… Edgar guy," I say. "He really freaked me out."

"There's no reason," Peter answers. "Every town has one."

"One Edgar?"

He smiles a charming smile. "One homeless guy. He's really quite nice, and sometimes he says really funny stuff."

"Yeah, funny." I think about what he said about the woman who no one sees, about my friend and the moon. A real comedian, that guy. "Why doesn't someone do something about him?"

Peter shrugs. "What should we do with him? Pack him in a crate and send him home? Edgar has no home. There is nowhere to send him to. I can call the police, ask them to handle it, but I don't want to do that. I tried to get him to leave the shopping mall once."

"And what happened?"

"He said that he'd tell me…" He falls silent.

"Tell you what?" I ask.

"Nothing. Just some nonsense. He just didn't want to leave."

I glance at Peter. He seems bothered by something. "He never harms anyone," he says again. Obviously Edgar managed to unnerve him as well, at least once. What did he tell him?

We walk silently for a little while. It's approaching noon, and the sun is baking the street mercilessly. Peter doesn't seem to mind. As far as I can tell he doesn't sweat at all. As we walk he looks around alertly, for anything out of the ordinary. Though of course, nothing is. Ordinary is the main theme here.

"Why does Narrowdale need security?" I ask. "It seems like a quiet place."

"Oh, it is." Peter nods. "I'm not sure why we were hired. My boss just said that we have to make sure that the residents are safe."

"Safe from what?"

"You know," he says. "Just… safe."

"That sounds strange."

"Are you new in Narrowdale?" Peter asks, clearly trying to change the subject.

"Yes. How did you know?"

"I didn't, but Edgar said… So what do you think of this place?"

"So far I pretty much hate it," I blurt out before I can help myself.

Peter seems a bit hurt. I bite my tongue but can't take my words back. We walk on wordlessly until we reach my new home.

"This is it," I say. "Thank you for walking with me."

"My pleasure," he says. "If Edgar gives you any trouble, don't take him seriously. He never–"

"Harms anyone," I say.

"That's right." Peter smiles. He really does have a beautiful smile. He says goodbye, and it takes me a few seconds to remember to say goodbye as well. Classy, Amy, really classy.

The door is unlocked, and I walk inside. Anthony is sitting in the kitchen, eating a peanut butter sandwich. No one loves peanut butter like Anthony does. He eats peanut butter for breakfast, lunch, and sometimes even for dinner. Before he went to college, Mom used to buy three large jars of peanut butter every week just for him. These days he comes home only occasionally, on weekends, so one jar is enough.

"Hi, Amy," he grins. "It looks like you've moved."

"We've moved," I say, stressing the "we" part. I don't care if he's in college. He still lives with us as far as I'm concerned. "What do you think?" I approach the cupboard to get a glass. I'm thirsty as hell.

"I like LA better."

"Me too. Just be glad you weren't here for all the cleaning and unpacking." I get the glass and pour myself some cold water from the fridge.

"Well, I noticed that you unpacked everything for me. Thanks." He rolls his eyes at me.

"With pleasure. What's a sister for?" I turn my back to him, putting the bottle back in the fridge.

"Sometimes it's just wonderful to have you around. It's hard to articulate with mere words how thankful I am for all your help with unpacking my stuff."

"No, really, it's fine. No need to thank me." I turn back to him and smile widely.

"Oh, no, I really appreciate it. In fact, I appreciated it so much I felt I just had to return the favor."

Damn. I dash upstairs to my room and open the closet. Everything seems to be in order. I open my underwear drawer. Empty.

"Anthony!!!"

"You don't have to shout. I'm right here," he says, standing in the doorway and munching on his sandwich. "You just organized my closet so nicely–"

"Where–"

"…I wanted to do the same for you, you know."

"Where's all my stuff?"

"Here and there," he answers, leaving the room. "Here and there."

God, he's so juvenile. I tear through my room, finding two pairs of panties under the bed. A quick search in my parents' room comes up with three more, and in the living room, under the TV, are two bras. I march into the kitchen with intention to kill. Anthony isn't there, but Mom is, preparing lunch. Hamburgers, Anthony's favorite.

"Hi, sweetie." She smiles. "Did you see that Anthony's home?"

"We've met, yes."

"Amy, why was your bra in the fridge?" She hands it over, raising an eyebrow.

"I have no idea."

"Okay," she says with a clear "I don't want to know" tone. "How was your day?"

Looking around for more places where my underwear could be, I sigh. "I don't know, Mom. It isn't over yet."

CHAPTER FOUR

I expected the first day of school would be awful, and it is certainly living up to my expectations. I have no one to talk to. Everybody's happy to see everybody else except for me, because nobody has a clue who I am. I try not to look pathetic as I walk down the hallway, looking desperately for my homeroom. Apparently its location was designed to be a complete mystery. I explore all the corridors of the school at least twice before the bell rings, signaling the beginning of the first class. First day, first class, already late. Well done, Amy.

Eventually, I find myself at a dead end. The corridor seemed to be so promising when I started following it, but it betrayed my trust, ending abruptly with no apparent door or passageway. The walls of this pointless passage are decorated with pictures of previous principals, pictures of the school in various times, yearbook photos of selected students. Despite the fact that I'm already late for my class, and getting later by the second, I find myself drawn to these pictures.

I walk by the last three principals of this school. The first two are looking with extreme seriousness towards the camera, one of them sporting the longest moustache I have ever seen. The third looks less serious. In fact, he almost seems to be laughing. Underneath his photo someone wrote on the glass with a marker "Stanley Brown – Went to check out the noise in the music room, and has never been seen since. Only in Narrowdale." Odd.

The fourth photo is of a teenager, a girl, probably a graduate. It's not very good. The entire photo is unfocused, so I can't really make out her features, and it looks like someone wandered into the picture, because there's a blurry kind of shadow standing behind her. The girl is probably some outstanding student, chosen to have her photo in this corridor. Some honor.

The next photo is of a group of graduates, and four adults who are probably teachers. Someone painted a red X on three of the students' faces, and on one of the teachers' faces as well. The next photo, also of some graduates, has two red X marks as well. Seems like pointless, tasteless vandalizing. I can understand adding a small beard or a pair of glasses, but this?

Okay Amy, let's get going. Wasting time in this corridor will get you nowhere.

Finally, fifteen minutes late, I locate my homeroom door, which I have already passed by twice, thinking it was a janitor's closet. I hesitantly knock, then enter, interrupting the teacher as she is talking. She frowns as she looks at me along with everyone else.

"Yes?" she asks.

"Hello, um… My name is Amy. I was assigned to this homeroom, but I couldn't find it and–"

"Amy Parker?"

"Yes."

"You just moved to Narrowdale, right?" says the teacher. "Principle Wright told me to expect you. Nice to meet you, Amy. What can you tell us about yourself?"

Hmmm, let's see. I don't like to be standing in front of thirty students, after being late and having to talk about myself, that's one thing. "Well, my name is Amy and I just… I mean, my family just moved here from Los Angeles. We moved a few days ago, so I am really new in Narrowdale and…" What else can I say about me? Nothing much. Fourteen years, and my entire existence can be summed up in one sentence. "And that's it, I guess."

"Well, welcome to Narrowdale, Amy."

Some of the students mumble half-hearted greetings.

"Please have a seat," the teacher continues.

Well, it isn't really have "a" seat, as much as "the only seat available". Apparently, the only chair left is one in the front, exactly in the middle. I hate sitting in front. I hate sitting in the middle. Well, life sucks. I sit down as the teacher carries on lecturing about her general expectations. I suddenly realize I have no idea what her name is. She probably introduced herself when the class started.

A cell phone rings. What idiot leaves his cell phone turned on during class? The teacher emphasizes that phones should be off. Everyone waits for the miscreant with the ringing phone to turn it off. It keeps ringing. Why are they staring at me? Right, it's my phone. I frantically rummage through my school bag, searching for my phone, stumbling on notebooks, books, pens, pencils… where is the damn phone? In a minute I'll start crying. Another ring, another one, the teacher coughs, another ring, there it is! Turn it off!

"From now on," says the teacher, "I don't want to hear or see any phones." She looks squarely at me when she says it. I can feel everyone's stares pointed at me. I look at the wall. Mustn't cry.

The teacher starts to drone on again, and the students' attention quickly wanders away from the degenerate new kid. I study the students around me, specifically the girls. To my left sits a girl with a tight green tank top and a black skirt. She has delicate makeup, and large silver hoop earrings dangle from her earlobes. She looks amazing, and next to her I feel drab and boring. My blue shirt suddenly feels as if I bought it from a discount stall in a third-rate mall. And why didn't I wear makeup? Back in LA I sometimes wore makeup, didn't I?

As the hour drags on, I daydream about happier times, when I knew everybody, and did not feel so awkward. When the bell rings I walk on to the next class in my schedule, math. There at least I am on familiar ground. I never understood math in LA either. After that comes Spanish–*odio la escuela!*–then Science class. After four hours I already pity myself quite thoroughly. Finally, lunch. I happily rummage through my bag to locate my lunch bag. Thank god I decided to prepare my own lunch. At least I won't have to eat the inedible cafeteria food on my first day. Except… I can't find it anywhere. I took it with me this morning, I'm almost certain! Well, I definitely remember seeing it on the kitchen table, and I can recall my intent of taking it…

I didn't take it.

I have no money for lunch, and the only thing I have to eat is an apple which I took from the fridge as an afterthought, thinking I might be hungry between classes. I take the lone, small apple in my hand, and follow the throng of students funneling into the cafeteria.

Ah, school cafeterias. Nothing like them to make the new, helpless student feel even more new and helpless. There is nothing worse than being alone during lunch. It is a mark of shame. It means that you've got no friends, you're at the bottom of the social food chain, and you're wasting the best years of your life.

All the tables are full of students who've apparently known each other since birth. The smells are unfamiliar and unappetizing. The harsh neon light makes me feel as if my deficiencies are enhanced tenfold. Empty seats beckon me, but the students around them all look unfriendly, hostile. Why aren't there any tables for one person? What sadistic, depraved mind created this hell on earth?

I locate a bunch of girls sitting around a table which has one empty seat. They look like the kind of girls I would normally associate with, no strange makeup, piercing or clothing. Fine, in I go. I approach them slowly.

"… and then yesterday we got back, stopping for six hours in Paris," says one of them, a redhead in a purple shirt.

"Really? Did you do anything there?" asks her friend, a blonde with a haircut similar to mine.

"Well, duh! Dad gave me his credit card, and we went shopping. I bought these gorgeous pair of sandals…"

"How much did they cost?"

"I don't know, maybe two hundred dollars, but they're totally worth it, and then I bought a white shirt which looks really good on me. I'll wear it tomorrow, you'll see."

"Hi," I say. "Can I sit here?"

The looks I am given make me feel like a bug on the wall. Never has the word "no" been so clearly stated.

"Of course," the redhead says with a tight-lipped smile.

I sit down, my eyes a bit lowered. I am already regretting my decision to join this table.

"I've been to Paris once," says one of them, continuing their conversation.

"When you were three," the redhead says pointedly.

"So what? I remember things."

"Of course you do. I'm sure your parents bought you the most classy chewing toys."

The girl shuts up, humiliated, as her friends laugh.

"So," the blonde asks the redhead. "What time did you get back?"

"We landed at four a.m. I totally crashed, I was so tired."

I decide to take the plunge. "Night-time flights are hard," I say. "Two years ago I got back from the East Coast with my family, and I was completely exhausted afterwards."

They all become silent and stare at me.

"Yeah," agrees one of them, a blonde with golden stud earrings. "They're hard."

"Hey," chirps the other one, a girl with a delicate face and short black hair. "What's your name again?"

"Amy," I answer. "Amy Parker."

"Right! I'm in your homeroom class. When did you say you moved to Narrowdale?"

"A couple of days ago. It was really intense. And worse of all, the air conditioner was broken, so the heat was just insufferable."

"Wow," says the blonde. "No air conditioner. That sucks."

"Anyway," says the redhead, clearly shutting me out. "You have to see the purse that my Dad got me in London. It's so awesome."

"Your Dad sure spoils you."

"Yeah, he loves buying me stuff."

"You know…," I start saying.

"Oh, and he got me a thin white gold bracelet. I'll show you tomorrow."

I take a small bite from my apple.

"Is that your lunch?" asks the girl with the black hair.

"Yeah," I say, embarrassed. "It's… I'm on a diet."

"Oh," she says. No one tries to say that I don't need the diet. I slowly begin to hate these girls.

I keep sitting next to them, nodding like I'm part of the conversation. I throw in a comment now and then, and they're polite, they don't interrupt me, but it's obvious that I don't belong. After a few minutes, I give up. I mumble something about going to the bathroom, and they smile at me, and keep on talking about the shopping they did during the summer vacation. I get up and leave. I walk a few steps. One of them says something softly, and they all burst out laughing. My face turns completely red. Maybe she wasn't talking about me, maybe she was talking about something else. But I know that she was talking about me, definitely talking about me. I feel humiliated.

Trying to repress my hurt feelings, I start looking for the bathroom. Apparently, this is not an easy task. In LA, I couldn't walk six feet without encountering numerous toilets, as far as the eye can see. Here they've hidden them. I can only presume this is a school policy, to allow only the students with the keenest eyes to find them.

Okay, Amy, time to ask for directions. The main hallway is crowded with students milling about. I notice the girl who was sitting next to me in class. She is walking on her own, making it feel safer to approach her.

"Hi, I'm Amy, I sat next to you in class."

"I'm Roxanne."

"Hey, Roxanne. I'm new in Narrowdale, I got here a week ago."

"Oh?"

"Yeah." I look at her expectantly, hoping she makes the next step in the conversation. This doesn't happen.

"Anyway…," I fumble. "Say, what's the name of our homeroom teacher? I guess I wasn't there when she introduced herself."

"Mrs. Smith. She said we can call her Abigail."

"Abigail, great. Listen, I just wanted to tell you, that tank top looks so good on you." I'm definitely babbling. What's happening to me? "I'm having some regrets about the clothes I chose this morning. I wanted to make a good first impression, but I don't know, I think it came out a little drab."

"Don't feel bad." She smiles at me. "Perhaps you'll do better tomorrow."

I glare at her, offended. She wasn't supposed to say that. She was supposed to say I look nice.

"I'm sorry," she says, embarrassed. She must have realized what I was thinking. "It's just that this shirt doesn't really look good on you; it makes your hips seem a bit wide. But your pants are really okay."

Oh, the compliments. "Where is the bathroom?" I ask weakly, tired of making a fool of myself. From now on I will keep my sentences to the minimum.

"Oh, it's just that way." She points. "You'll see it."

I thank her. As I walk towards the bathroom, I do my best to put on my busy face. That's why I'm not talking to anyone right now, I'm simply going somewhere really important. I'm not that girl who hangs around alone.

There's a kid about my age leaning against the wall, filming something with a video camera. When I walk by him, he points the camera straight at me. I turn my head away and walk faster. What the hell is he filming me for?

I find the girls' bathroom and go inside one of the stalls. I'm not coming out until lunch is over. When the school bell rings I go to my next class, English. I sit in one of the chairs, and a moment later Roxanne enters the class and sits next to me. I do my best to ignore her.

CHAPTER FIVE

During the next few hours my hunger becomes acute. I'm feeling weak, and my head is spinning a bit. Truth is, I didn't have any breakfast, and yesterday evening I barely ate because I was so stressed about the first day of school... The bell shatteringly proclaims the end of the day. We didn't have a bell back in LA. We had music playing over the intercom. I'd always hated the tunes blaring at us from all the school corners, but now I miss them wholeheartedly.

Everyone pushes their way out. I wait until the room is empty, and then I get up.

On the way out I get dizzy, and suddenly I lose my balance. Someone grabs my arm.

"Are you okay?"

It's him, the jerk with the video camera. I don't know him at all, of course, but I decide that everything is his fault. The crappy day I had, my missing lunch bag, my ringing cell, the bitches in the cafeteria, my parents moving us to this hellhole without even making sure the air conditioner works. It's all because of him.

"I'm fine," I snap, yanking my arm away.

"For a second there you looked as if you were about to faint," he mumbles, staring at the sidewalk.

"I'm okay. Leave me alone." I turn my back on him and walk swiftly away.

Leaving the school gate behind me, I start feeling a bit ashamed. He didn't really do anything. Actually, it was kind of nice of him to stop me from doing a face plant on the sidewalk. But I decide that the best course of action is to ignore the guilt and engross myself in anger and resentment instead. It feels much more satisfying.

I get on the school bus. The only seat left is one by a window. The girl that sits next to it is leaning across the aisle talking to her friends. I approach the seat, and notice that her schoolbag is on it.

"Excuse me," I say.

She ignores me, whispering with her friends, who are giggling uncontrollably.

"Excuse me," I say more loudly. "Can you move your bag, please?"

She becomes silent and stares at me, her eyes brimming with hatred. I guess she recognizes me as the one who murdered her parents and burned her house down, because I can see no other justification for her hateful look. She removes her bag in a sharp movement meant to show that it is the worst thing that I could have asked. I sigh and step over her. I accidentally step on her foot, and the seething look she gives me as I finally sit down would have made me squirm, if I still cared.

The school bus makes a strange and twisting journey all around town, and I manage to lose my bearings. I slowly get the feeling that it already drove past my stop, and I've forgotten to get off. I can already picture myself staying last on the bus, the driver staring at me, asking "Excuse me, what–"

Hang on? What's that? This looks familiar! I think this is my stop! I get up abruptly, pushing past the girl sitting next to me without saying anything. She and her friends can all drop dead, as far as I am concerned. I get off the bus just as the doors are closing.

It's the wrong stop.

I look around, my eyes scanning identical-looking houses, a small park with a red slide and two yellow swings, some tired-looking trees. I think I know where I am. This is actually one of the streets that I passed when Peter walked me home. My house is about a ten-minute walk from here, not that bad. If it only wasn't so hot…

When I finally manage to drag myself to our front door, I feel like a rag doll. I'm hungry, exhausted, upset. I'm pretty sure that once I walk inside and my Mom asks me how my day was, I might start crying. I lean on the door, twisting the door handle…

The door is locked. There is no one home. Of course.

"Forgot your key?" The voice makes me jump in surprise. I twist and look at the speaker. It's Alex, our next-door neighbor. He is wearing the same jeans that I saw him with last time and a white t-shirt with a faded brown stain. He's standing on his porch, looking at me. Was he there before? I don't know.

"Yeah, I…" In fact, I don't think I have a key yet. Mom didn't give me one. "I guess I did."

"Want to come inside my place?" he asks "It's hot out here."

I stare at him in disbelief. Does he really think I'd walk inside a stranger's house? "No, thanks," I answer. "I… My Mom will be here any minute."

"Suit yourself." He shrugs and walks back to his house. His dog is sitting in his yard, looking at me and panting. I pull out my phone and call Mom.

"Hey sweetie!"

"Mom! Where are you?"

"I just got my hair done at the local hairdresser. He did such a nice job! And much cheaper than in LA."

"Mom, I just got home, and I don't have a key!"

"Oh you're already home? Sorry, sweetie, I was sure I had a bit more time. I'll be home in ten minutes."

It actually takes her more than fifteen. When she finally gets home, I'm dehydrated as well. This has been the worst day. Ever.

CHAPTER SIX

I'm walking down the dark street. Why aren't the streetlights working? In the distance, a dog howls morosely and then starts barking. My footsteps echo eerily in the silent neighborhood. There is something deeply unpleasant about the surrounding darkness, and I decide to walk faster. What is that noise? Someone whistling? It's just my imagination. The only sounds are my steps and the dog barking. Soon I'll be home. I have a strange feeling that someone is following me, but I don't want to look back. I quicken my pace even more. Is the dog barking louder, or am I simply getting closer? My throat tightens, my heart is pounding, I start running. It's so hot, why am I wearing a coat? Is someone chasing me? My ankle twists, I trip…

I open my eyes, gasping. A dream. Of course it was a dream. Only the dog's barking lingers on. I get out of bed and approach the window. The white dog is standing in Alex's backyard, barking angrily into the darkness. It seems to notice me, whines, and becomes silent.

I glance at the clock. It's thirty-seven minutes past three. No way am I falling asleep again, not with the stifling heat in my room, not after that dream. Yuck, I'm sweating. Tomorrow it ends. Tomorrow…

Hunger creeps up on me. I stumble downstairs to the kitchen, fantasizing about a peanut-butter-and-jelly sandwich. My hand meets with the fridge's door, brushes across several magnets, locates the handle, and pulls it. The harsh white light shoots out, instantly blinding me. I stand dazed, trying to understand who I am, where I am. Finally I recover and spot the desired jelly jar. I pick it up, get the sliced bread and the peanut butter, and make myself a small heavenly sandwich. Following this rejuvenating snack, I'm feeling much better. My eyes spot the storage room's door. At night, in the darkness, it's much more threatening. My throat feels dry, and I force myself to look away, ignore the door looming in the shadows. I drink a glass of cold water, followed by another. Now I need to pee. Off to the bathroom. The flushing seems to be much louder when everyone is asleep. I go back to bed without brushing my teeth, because I am a disgusting, lazy girl.

Forty-nine minutes past three. Almost three and a half hours till morning. Knowing myself, I'll probably fall asleep fifteen minutes before the alarm clock goes off. I don't know how I'll manage to survive tomorrow with so little sleep. Someone is whistling outside. Who walks around whistling so late at night? Now the dog starts barking again. Fantastic.

My footsteps echo in the darkness. I look around, noticing that the streetlights aren't working. I shove my hands down my coat's pockets. It's hot, this coat doesn't make sense. A dog is barking in the distance. Is someone following me? Couldn't be, no one walks around here at this hour. Why am I running? Soon I'll be home, I'm really close. Where is my home? Someone is chasing me, I can hear him huffing. Mustn't stop, mustn't stop, one of my ankles twists and I trip. A hand grabs my hair...

This time I scream as I wake up. I lift my hand quickly to fight off the stranger and realize that it was just another dream. It's ten minutes past five. Instead of going back to sleep I go and take a shower. We moved a week ago, and I've already taken more than twenty showers.

I get out of the shower and try to decide what to wear. This time, I'm going to really do my best. I have time to compose myself, and it's my chance to show the girls in my class that I'm a cool girl from LA who they want to be friends with. No! Who they must be friends with, because if you're not my friend, you don't exist! No more Amy with a drab blue shirt! I put on the dark denim shorts I bought last year for the live concert Nicole and I went to. A green shirt with a thin brown belt that Mom bought me in New York matches the shorts perfectly. I put on a pearl-shaded lipstick and some mascara. Wow, I'm looking good. I should get up every morning at five.

I make myself a bowl of cereal, take it upstairs to my room and sit down in front of my laptop. Nothing interesting is happening on the Internet. I contemplate uploading another post to my blog and realize I've got nothing to say. Jennifer Scott shared two links. Video clips of cats. Almost everything she shares consists of cats in one way or another.

I hate cats.

My eyes slowly shut and I nod off for a couple of minutes in front of the screen. I wake up with a panicky feeling, and a frantic glance at the laptop screen discloses that I am horribly late. Damn! Why didn't Mom or Dad wake me up? If I don't leave right now, I will be late for the school bus. I run downstairs, and spot a note and some money left on the table. I quickly read Mom's words: "Sweetie, I had to leave early for a job interview. I didn't have time to pack lunch for you, so just buy something in the school cafeteria. And Amy–if I find out that you bought a skirt with the money and went hungry all day like last year, I will make you eat that skirt. I will cook it nicely, with some vegetables and rice. I will call it 'Skirt a la mode.' Have a nice day!" I snatch the money, shove it into my school bag and dash outside. Cursing myself, I can already imagine the frustration of being late on the only morning I've ever woken up before dawn. I run all the way to the bus stop, manage to get there just in time, and hop on the bus. Katie, a girl from my Spanish class, is sitting in one of the front seats. She looks at me, raises an eyebrow and whispers something to her friend, who snickers. They don't seem to be admiring my cooler-than-cool appearance.

I sit in front of them, trying to ignore the creeping feeling that they're talking about me. What's with you, Amy? The world does not revolve around you. People have other things in their life besides you.

"… Jane told me she saw her talking to the homeless guy who hangs around the shopping center…," I hear Katie whisper to her friend. Great. I'm sure she wanted me to hear that. No one whispers this loud.

"Perhaps they have some common interests?" suggests her friend.

"Their taste in clothing?" says Katie, and they both burst out laughing.

No. I won't let those bitches hurt me. These aren't tears, I'm just tired. I dry my eyes in a swift movement (tears? What tears?) and take a deep breath. I'm Amy Parker, the coolest girl to ever step in this god forsaken pathetic place. They'll see.

As soon as we get to school, I duck into the bathroom and inspect myself in the mirror. My face is red and sweaty due to my forced morning run, and my eyes are decorated with dark circles. My mascara got smeared, probably because of the sweat on my face. I suddenly recall that I haven't brushed my teeth this morning (not to mention after my midnight snack). How did I come to this sorry state? I wash my face and wet my hair a little. I don't look like an accident anymore, but I'm not America's next top model either. I am a tired girl who tried to dress cool, and didn't really manage to.

Math class drags slowly. The lesson is about… something. Something, which, when combined with something else, creates a third something, but we mustn't use the fourth something because… it's bad for some reason. I try to concentrate on the words leaving the teacher's mouth, but quickly they become a jumble of meaningless syllables. I nearly fall asleep three times. I should have stayed home. Today the air conditioning will be fixed. I will finally have a good night's sleep. Math is followed by Science and I start to wonder if life is really worth the bother. By the third period I am not even sure what class I am in. I consult my schedule and simply shuffle to the correct classroom.

Finally, the bell saves us all. I leave the class, once more by myself. I stand in the cafeteria line and buy some… for lack of a better word, food. There is overcooked pasta. There are drab, unhappy vegetables. There is a purple wobbly thing with strange pieces of something on top. I wonder if Mom's "skirt a la mode" might taste better after all. I decide to avoid the girls I sat with on Friday. I locate an empty chair and quickly sit. Looking around at the occupants of the other chairs, I quickly realize that I've sat down with a bunch of emo girls. Sullen, unfriendly stares fix on me. This diminishes my appetite even more than the cafeteria's food does, and after nibbling on some pasta, I lay down my fork and simply stare vacantly at the tray. I wake up to the sound of laughter. A couple of the girls are looking at me, grinning. Apparently, I dozed off. Needless to say, falling asleep during lunch will not make me the coolest girl in school. I stand up and start walking towards the cafeteria's exit, alone. I must find myself someone to be with, someone to talk to.

Hang on, that guy over there is the guy with the vidcam. I pause and sneak a look at him.

He is thin with curly, dark hair and a pasty white complexion. His neck is pinkish, probably due to careless exposure to the sun. He is dressed in a plain white T-shirt and jeans. His sneakers seem to be a bit worn out. He is looking at his camera with intense concentration, ignoring the uneaten cafeteria food in front of him. The chairs to his left and right are empty. Two boys with glasses are sitting across from him, talking to each other.

I sit down to his left. Why? Guilt? Maybe just my own selfish need to be seen with another student? Perhaps an actual desire to meet someone? There is no way to be sure. Both boys on the other side of the table look at me for a second, then resume their quiet conversation, ignoring me. The boy with the camera glances my way, then goes back to his tinkering. Not very inviting, but then again, I definitely earned it.

"Hi." I keep looking at him, and repeat the same sentence I've been saying over and over these past two days. "I haven't introduced myself. My name is Amy. I'm new here."

"Shane," he says without raising his head.

"Look, I... I'm sorry I was kind of nasty yesterday. I just didn't feel so well, and I had a really crappy day, and... that's it. You know. I'm sorry."

"Okay." He aims his camera at me.

"Please don't," I say, a bit irritated.

He lowers the camera and looks at me, raising his eyebrows. "You don't like to be filmed?"

I shrug. Who likes to be filmed by strangers? "What's with the camera?"

"I like filming videos."

"Me too. But I use my phone to do that, like everyone else does."

"I like filming with a video camera," he says. "The film's quality is much better."

"Whatever. I have great clips that I took with my phone."

"Okay."

"What grade are you?" I ask, changing the subject.

"Ninth."

"Really? Me too!" I say. "I wonder if we share any classes."

"I haven't seen you in any of my classes," he remarks.

"Well... it's only been a day and a half."

"That's true. So... you're new to this school?"

"Yup."

"Where did you live before?"

"In LA. We moved to Narrowdale a week ago."

"Yeah? What do you think of it so far?"

I hesitate, remembering Peter's reaction. "I don't know... I'm new here."

"I hate this place," he says.

He's kind of negative, this Shane. But then again, I also hate this place, so who am I to judge?

"Why do you hate it?" I ask.

He laughs. "You'll see, this place sucks. Did you know there's a game called 'Only in Narrowdale'?"

"What do you mean?"

"You take turns saying a sentence beginning with the words 'only in Narrowdale'. For example, only in Narrowdale is there no bus to LA."

"And who wins?"

"No one. We all live in Narrowdale. We all lose. Only in Narrowdale is there a classroom in the school which no one ever enters."

"What? What do you mean?"

"Only in Narrowdale…" he repeats, and pauses. "There's an entire classroom in the high school which is always empty. No one ever enters it."

"Yeah, really? Uh… Oh." I finally get it. "Are we playing 'Only in Narrowdale' right now?"

He smiles and starts fiddling with his camera again.

"Only in Narrowdale..." I furrow my brow. "Only in Narrowdale is there a homeless guy near the shopping mall who no one does anything about."

"Actually, I think this is a very common problem in our country." He thinks for a second. "Only in Narrowdale does the mayor break a mirror each morning."

"Really?"

He shrugs.

"Only in Narrowdale... do people play the game 'Only in Narrowdale.'" I feel disgustingly pleased with myself. I've beaten the system. Ha!

The bell rings. Shane gets up. "See?" he says. "You've become a local already." He picks up his tray and walks away. What a weird guy.

But at least I had someone to talk to during lunch.

http://amy.strangerealm.com/nightmares.html

CHAPTER SEVEN

Friday noon, algebra lesson. Mrs. Mermenstein, the teacher, is talking about parabolas while writing on the whiteboard, her back to the class. Students around me whisper to each other. I have no whispering companion, no murmuring ally. To my left sits a girl whose name I don't know, but I've already decided I can't stand her. To my right, an empty seat. Behind me sits Josh, a weirdo with huge glasses and an uninviting odor. Next to him, Jasmine, whom I also can't stand. In fact, it seems I can't stand most of the girls in my math class.

How many nights have I passed sleepless? Four? Five? Mrs. Mermenstein's dry voice and the air conditioner's humming make me feel sleepy. Instead of copying the writing on the whiteboard, I am scribbling doodles as far as the eye can see. The page is covered with circles, squares, butterflies, flowers, wavy lines, stars, dots... oodles of doodles.

"Amy!" Mrs. Mermenstein says sharply, making me raise my head in surprise.

"Yes?"

"Can you please tell me what the meeting point of the parabola and the y axis is?"

Meeting point. Parabola. y. Why oh why.

"The meeting point?" I stall. My eyes roam the whiteboard in panic. There are many things on it that might be parabolas.

"Yes, what is the meeting point?"

"With the axis of–"

45

"With the y axis."

The phrase $y = 13x^2 - 26$ is written on the whiteboard's top left corner. Is that a parabola? I have a hunch that it might very possibly be so. When does it meet the y axis? How can one even divine such knowledge? "Uh... thirteen?" I hedge.

Mrs. Mermenstein sighs audibly. "How did you come up with that marvelous number?"

"I..." Sometimes it's just better to give up. "I don't know."

"You don't know?"

"No."

"You just guessed the number thirteen?"

"I thought that the answer might be thirteen." I shift uncomfortably.

"Well!" she says sharply. "If Amy's vast knowledge of parabolas is an example, it seems that you all need a lot more practice. Before our next lesson I would like you all to solve problems three to seventeen. I will check your notebooks, so I suggest you do it seriously." The bell rings, punctuating her sentence ominously, and she stalks out of the classroom before any of us can get up.

"Thanks, Amy," The nameless girl to my left hisses at me as she is shoving her notebook into her bag. "Are you really that stupid, or are you just pretending? Was it that hard to look at the board and answer the question?"

I watch her silently. I have nothing to say. Tears are running up my throat, I mustn't cry. She turns her back on me and storms out of the class.

"You could have just said you don't know the answer," says Jasmine as she is walking out. Her friend, Carley, just sends a contemptuous look towards me, saying nothing. Mustn't cry.

"Thanks, Amy, really," says some guy whose name I don't recall.

Slowly the class empties. I stay seated, as if glued to my chair. My notebook is covered with useless shapes. The whiteboard is also covered with letters and numbers, mocking me and my stupidity, challenging me to answer the unanswered question. Mustn't cry. I'll cry at home.

"Amy?" someone says behind me. I ignore her. She'll only say something mean to me, too.

"Amy." The girl sits next to me. "You really shouldn't let Mrs. Mermenstein get under your skin. She's a real bitch. She's nasty to everyone."

I raise my eyes. It's one of the quiet girls in class. Another girl whose name I don't know.

"I..." They are coming fast, the tears. Mustn't cry. I bite my lip. "It's not her." My voice is shaking. I'm breathing heavily. I am not about to cry.

"Then why are you..." She looks at me with concern. "You just seem a bit... a bit hurt."

"I have to go." I stand up quickly, grabbing my notebook and my bag, practically running out of the class. My eyes are lowered, tears running silently down my face. I do my best to avoid being seen. I won't take the school bus today. In fact, I should go to the bathroom first. I turn and collide with someone.

"Amy?" It's her again. The quiet girl. What does she want? I ignore her, not wanting to embarrass myself by crying in front of her. I walk to the bathroom, enter one of the stalls, and begin to cry. I haven't cried since the first day in Narrowdale. I feel all of the pent-up frustration and anger and misery release at once. I cry for a whole five minutes, a liberating and unrestrained weeping, with tears and moans and snot.

Finally I calm down. I breathe deeply, leave the stall, and wash my face. I stare at the mirror. My nose is a bit red, and so are my eyes, but if no one looks at me closely (and let's face it; no one here does) I guess I'm fine.

I leave the bathroom and stop in my tracks. On the bench in the hallway sits that girl from my math class. Her hair is auburn and long, almost down to her hips. A faded black shirt, a little too wide. Nondescript jeans. Pink sandals. Her face is delicate, and has something sweet in it. If she would only try, she could be beautiful, maybe even gorgeous. But the way she dresses, her haircut and her body language make her one of those girls whom no one seems to notice.

What is she doing here? Is she stalking me? She smiles at me. That's a refreshing experience, someone smiling at me. Feeling better, I try to smile back.

"Are you okay?" she asks.

"I… Yeah, I guess so," I answer, wondering what she wants.

"You were feeling hurt."

"Yes, but not because of that witch."

"Then by who?" She looks confused.

"All the assholes in our class."

She stands up. "Why?"

"I don't feel like talking about it. Listen, no offense but... I don't remember your name."

"Coral."

"Coral," I say. "Hang on, aren't you in my homeroom?"

"Yeah, and also in social studies and English."

"Oh," I say embarrassed.

"Well, you're the new girl, so it's easier to notice you."

I nod. "Um… Were you waiting for me?"

"Yeah, I wanted to make sure that you are all right."

I pause for a second. Why is she so nice to me?

"I am," I finally say.

"I'm glad."

"Thanks for waiting."

"You're welcome. Say, do you need some help with the math homework?"

"No," I quickly say, then stop. Maybe she's really just a shy girl, trying to be nice. Would it hurt to try being friendly? "Um... Well, actually, I do. I'm not sure I know what a parabola is. Unless it's some kind of Italian pasta."

"Okay." Coral laughs. "I'd be glad to help."

"Great, thanks." I'm unsure what else to say.

She smiles shyly. "Would you like to meet during the weekend and do the homework together?"

"Uh…" Meet? Are we already in the 'invite each other home' phase? "Okay. Sure. Let's do that."

CHAPTER EIGHT

"So, if x equals zero," says Coral. "What do we get?"

"If x equals zero...," I answer slowly.

"Yes?"

"Then x is zero."

"Right."

"It's nothing. Nada."

"Yes. And then what is the point of intersection?"

"Um, what equation are we looking at?"

Coral sighs. "Amy, you're not very focused."

"No, no, I'm very focused." I yawn. I didn't sleep again last night. I'm on the brink of collapse. "This is just so interesting, I have to solve all the questions at once. I'm too focused, that's the real problem. Let's take a break."

"We just took a break."

"Sunday morning is a very bad time to do homework."

"You have a better time?"

"Sure! Monday afternoon. Next month."

"Okay, look." Coral puts down her pen and looks at me intently. "We'll do two more. And then we'll take a break. A short break."

"Promise?"

"Yes. But it'll be a really short break. And I want you to solve the questions on scrap paper, and not in your notebook."

"But then I have to copy them all to my notebook. It's so inefficient!" I complain.

"Yes, but then your notebook won't look like the scrawled notes of a patient in a mental institute."

"What's wrong with the way my notebook looks?" I protest.

We both contemplate my notebook. My first attempt didn't go so well, so I crossed it out. Then, in the next question, I made a mistake near the end, so I tried to erase it, and the page creased and tore. At the beginning of the third question I got bored and started drawing little stars. One of them has a smiley face. Coral looks as if my notebook is giving her indigestion.

"It's perfectly fine," I mutter.

"Two questions on scrap paper," she says. "Then we'll take a twenty-minute break."

Mom walks in with two glasses of ice-cold water. "Hey, girls." She smiles "You're studying really hard!"

Mom didn't believe it at first when I told her a friend was coming over to study. She just said, "To do what?" and burst laughing, as if it was the best joke ever.

"Yes!" I whine, my voice full of despair. "Very hard!"

"Perhaps you should take a small break?" Mom suggests.

"Truth is...," Coral starts.

"Yes!" I say happily. "Coral, that's exactly what we need! A short break!"

"Amy..."

"I'm sure that a small break will help you focus. I can make some popcorn," Mom offers generously.

"Mom, you are completely right. A thirty-minute break will help us study so much better."

Coral's eyes glint with murderous intent. "Fine," she says. "Twenty minutes."

"I'll make popcorn," Mom says cheerfully and leaves the room.

"After that we solve ten questions," Coral snarls. "All on scrap paper."

"Oh, sure, naturally," I say innocently. "Just a very short, twenty-minute break."

We walk downstairs and sit down in the living room. Mom brings us a bowl of popcorn.

"I like your home," Coral says with her mouth full.

"Yeah?" I say. "I guess it's okay."

"It's really nice. I like your mom's taste in furniture."

Mom's taste in furniture usually revolves around whatever she found on sale, but I let it slide. Anthony walks in, wearing a sleeveless shirt and boxer shorts. He looks as if he just woke up.

"Good morning," I say. "Anthony, this is Coral, my friend, who didn't want to see your shorts."

He blinks and glances at her, amused. "How do you know that she didn't want to see them?" he asks and leaves the room.

"Sorry," I say. "That's my brother."

"It's fine," answers Coral, her face completely red. "I didn't know you had a brother."

"Yeah, sorry. He usually wears more clothes." I pause to think about it. "Well, actually, that's not really true. He occasionally wears more clothes."

Anthony walks in again, this time wearing pants.

"How can you sleep in this god-awful heat?" he asks me.

"I can't."

"I was awake all night!"

"I haven't slept for over a week."

"Coral, right?" he addresses Coral.

"Um... yes, that's right," she says.

"It's nice to meet you. I'm Anthony." He smiles. "So you're the one helping Amy with math?"

"I... we're studying together."

He bursts out laughing and leaves the room.

"Moron," I mutter.

"He seems nice," Coral says. "It must be fun, having an older brother."

"Just as fun as going to the dentist," I sigh. "He isn't actually here most of the time. He's at college."

"Oh."

"Do you have any siblings?"

"I have Mia," she answers.

"What is a Mia?"

"Mia's my baby sister. She's really young, only four years old, so we can't really talk. I wish I had a big brother."

"Take it from me, it's overrated."

"Okay." She gets up, brushing popcorn crumbs off her shorts. "Come on, we have to go back."

"Must we?"

"You promised."

"Fine, fine," I groan. What a waste of a nice Sunday morning.

CHAPTER NINE

Scrap paper covers my entire desk. I solve a problem, then another. Piles of problems. I am not sure how long I've been doing this. Two hours? Three? Two days? Perhaps five? I stare at the current problem. It's question number seven thousand eight hundred fifty-six. This has completely blown out of proportion. Up to what question did Mrs. Mermenstein say we had to solve? I sigh and put down my pencil.

The doorbell rings. Who can it be? Who rings a doorbell this late at night? Must be friends of Mom and Dad, maybe Anthony's. I wait, but no one answers the door. The doorbell rings once more.

I have to do everything around here. I go out of my room, walk down the stairs, and approach the main door.

"Who is it?"

No one answers. I open the door. There is no one outside. In the distance, down the street I can hear whistling. It's cool outside, pleasant. Inside the house it's stifling hot, as always. Why am I even standing in the doorway? Oh, right, the doorbell. Who was it? I step out.

The streetlights aren't working. There must be some problem. Never mind, there's light above our front door. I glance back. Where is our front door? It's the wrong street, I have to go back home. I quicken my steps. I'll be home soon.

It's quiet in the street, and cold. Really cold. It's a good thing I wore my coat. Someone is whistling behind me, a strange tune, screeching and unpleasant. Where did I hear this tune before? I stride faster, trying to get away from the whistling, but it only gets stronger, as if the person whistling is getting closer. I don't want to meet him, whoever he is. I start running. I'll be home in a minute, I'm nearly there. I can hear his footsteps getting closer. Who is it? He stops whistling, I can hear him huffing. It's so cold, the freezing air is hurting my lungs, but I mustn't stop, mustn't stop. My ankle twists, I trip, he grabs my hair… A hoarse whisper in my ear "Don't cry, sweetheart…"

"Amy?"

I'm shivering in my bed, my shaking hands clutching at my blanket. Outside my window I hear the whistling from my dream. How come none of the neighbors have reported this guy to the police by now?

"Amy." I hear Anthony outside my room. "Is everything okay?"

"Yes," I manage answering. "I'm fine."

"Can I come in?"

"Sure." I try not to sound too eager. "Come in, no problem."

Anthony opens the door and walks in. He's wearing a worn-out white t-shirt, and a pair of blue shorts. He doesn't look as if I woke him up. He was probably watching TV, as he often does on Sunday nights.

"I heard you yelling. Did you have a bad dream?"

"Yes."

"Is it that dream where you're swimming in the Olympics, and you suddenly realize that you forgot your swimming suit and you're completely naked?"

"No. I shouldn't have told you about that dream."

"No, you really shouldn't have," he agrees. "Do you want me to stay around for a bit?"

"You probably need to sleep."

He shrugs. "I have to get up in three hours anyway. I'll sleep at college."

"Okay, if you can stay here for a little while, it'll be nice," I say, surprisingly relieved. When we were younger, Anthony used to babysit me when our parents went out. I always had trouble going to sleep when Mom wasn't at home, but Anthony would tell me bedtime stories and stay by my bed until I fell asleep. We used to be much closer, I suddenly realize, a little sadly.

He glances at my window, where the whistling is coming from. "Perhaps I should close this?" he offers.

"No, leave it. If you close the window there's no air at all."

"Right." He sits on my chair. "So what did you dream about?"

"It was a crappy dream. I don't want to talk about it."

"It wasn't the one with the Smurfs, was it?"

"You know what? Maybe it's better that you go away and let me sleep."

"I'll be quiet," he says.

"Thanks." I shut my eyes.

"No Smurf shall pass without my noticing."

"Idiot," I mumble. Slowly I nod off into a deep and dreamless sleep.

CHAPTER TEN

"I can't believe she didn't check our notebooks," I mutter, brimming with self-righteous anger.

"What difference does it make?" Coral says.

"I worked so hard! I used scrap paper!"

"So what? Amy, do you think Mrs. Mermenstein would be impressed if she knew how hard you worked?" Coral laughs.

"I don't know. Well… yes! Doesn't it piss you off? We spent three hours yesterday on this shitty assignment!"

We enter the cafeteria. We both have lunch bags, so we look around for a table. I try to conceal my joy at the fact that I have someone to sit with. A friend! I don't need to find a table with one empty seat next to a bunch of hostile students. I can just sit with the people that my new friend sits with.

"Where do you usually sit?" I ask.

She shrugs. "Wherever."

Damn. No other friends, then. Still, two are better than one. I notice Shane sitting by himself, filming a couple of guys throwing food at each other.

"Hey, Shane!" I approach him, Coral tagging along. He points his camera towards us, and I make a face. He turns it off.

"What's up?" he says.

"Nothing much," I say. "Can we join you?"

"Sure."

"Great, thanks." We both sit in front of him, and I start opening my lunch bag. I notice Shane's raising one eyebrow, seemingly waiting for something.

"Oh, right," I finally say, a bit nervously. "Shane, this is Coral. Coral, this is Shane."

"Yo." He smiles at her. She smiles back. So far so good.

"What are you filming?" she asks.

"Nothing." He shoves the camera into its pouch. He looks at me. "You look tired."

"Nah, I just figured that black rings under the eyes look good on me."

"Really?"

"No. Not really. I am having a hard time sleeping lately." I look inside my lunch bag. Mom's made me a really nice peanut-butter-and-jelly sandwich. I take a bite. Mmmmm... good.

"How come?" Shane asks.

"Hmmmf?"

"How come you can't sleep?"

I swallow my bite. "Well, the air conditioner at my home works now, but it's kind of noisy. It's really hard to sleep when it's on, so my mom turns it off, and then it's hot as hell. But that's not the real problem..." I shiver when I remember last night's dream. The hand on my hair, and that creepy whisper, "Don't cry, sweetheart..."

"I have really weird nightmares," I carry on, "like, every night."

"What kind of nightmares?"

"The scary kind," I answer, annoyed. Why is he prying? I take another bite. Shane seems satisfied with my answer, but I find that I'm not. They're not just "the scary kind." They are repetitive. They are incredibly realistic, and in some ways they feel almost... foreign. As if it isn't really me in the dream. While I chew, I try to make sense of it all. The cold, the coat, the unfamiliar street...

"I dream I'm being chased," I blurt, unable to help myself.

"Chased by whom?" Coral furrows her brow.

"I have no idea," I answer uncomfortably. "But it's in a dark street, and it's cold..."

"And then what happens?" asks Shane.

"He catches me." I finish my sandwich and clean the crumbs from my hands. "And that's not the only creepy thing. There's whistling."

"Whistling? What kind of whistling?"

"You know, whistling. Someone's whistling outside in the street. Almost every night."

"Someone's whistling outside your window?" asks Coral. "Like 'Hey there' whistles?"

"Hey what?" Shane looks confused.

"Hey there, sexy," she says, as if it clarifies everything.

"What are 'Hey there, sexy' whistles?"

"Come on, you know. Hey there, sexy, nice rack!" she shouts and lets out a shrill whistle. A girl sitting nearby turns around in confusion. Shane and I burst out laughing.

"Not that kind of whistling," I explain. "It's as if someone is whistling some kind of strange tune. I don't think he's whistling it specifically at me. He just does it near my window."

"But who is it?"

"Shane, I have no clue," I say impatiently. "I don't walk outside in my pajamas, searching for strangers who whistle in the street. I'm not insane."

"You could ask your parents to check it out."

"I think not."

"I can come by and have a look."

I stare at him, uncomprehending.

"If someone's whistling outside your window every night, he could very well be trying to harass you. I could drop by and check it out."

I keep on staring. Does he really think I want him popping by my house in the middle of the night?

"No, thanks," I finally say. "It's nothing. We have to go, our next class is starting."

"There's still some time," Coral says.

"No, we really should go. We don't want to be late for our English class. You know how nasty she can be when students are running late." I get up. Coral looks at me in surprise, but stands up as well.

"Okay. Coral, it was nice meeting you," Shane says.

"You too. Bye."

"There are five more minutes until the bell rings," Coral whispers as we walk away. "Why did you say we have to go?"

"I don't know, I just didn't want to stay there. What a weirdo!" I shake my head in frustration. "I hardly know him. Why the hell is he proposing to rescue me in the middle of the night? Don't you think it's odd?"

"I think it was nice of him to offer."

"I don't know. He's weird."

"I think he's cute."

I glance at her in surprise. "Shane?"

"Yeah. Doesn't he seem cute to you?"

"He's... what?"

"I think he's cute," she says again.

"Whatever."

"Hey, Amy. If you ever want to talk... you know. About your dreams and all that, you can always call me."

I feel myself blushing. It's surprising, the way a little kindness can make me feel so good. "Great, thanks."

"My pleasure."

The remainder of the day drags by. As I walk between classes, I try and do it as fast as possible, to avoid running into Shane in the hallway. I don't want to risk his suggesting he swing by my house in the middle of the night. Finally the last bell rings, and another school day ends.

Walking outside with Coral, I notice Shane getting on the school bus. "You know what?" I say to Coral. "I think I'll walk today."

"Are you insane? It's like a thousand degrees outside."

"It's actually kind of pleasant."

"Sure. If you're a camel," she answers. "I'm going on the bus."

"You're just lazy."

"You're just nuts. See you tomorrow." She waves goodbye.

I start walking, choosing a route that doesn't go near the shopping mall and Edgar. Wonderful, my entire decision process is based on people I'm trying to avoid.

The sound of my footsteps reminds me of the dreams I've been having for the past couple of days. The fast pace, the short, frightened breaths, the mysterious shadow following me… My heart begins thumping. A hand grabs my hair, and the hoarse whisper…

"Hi!"

I nearly pee my pants in fright. I was so busy thinking about my dreams that I hadn't noticed Peter, the security guy, walking on the other side of the street. He smiles at me and continues walking.

The day's improving, no doubt about it. I cross the road and run after him, catching up quickly.

"Peter!" I smile. "How are you doing?"

"Fine," he answers. "How are you…" He suddenly stops. He doesn't remember my name. Well, the day's becoming irritating again.

"Amy," I remind him "My name is Amy."

"Right! How are you doing, Amy?"

I can't sleep at nights, our air conditioner sounds like a leaf blower and I hate this place. "I'm just great! So, maintaining order?"

He grins. "Actually, my shift is over, I'm going home to sleep. I'm patrolling again tonight."

"Oh." I nod, disappointed. I was hoping he'd escort me home again. "All night?"

"Midnight to six AM," he answers.

"Say." Something suddenly occurs to me. "Do you whistle while you patrol?"

"Whistle?" He looks at me in confusion.

"Yeah. Like, this funny tune." I whistle the tune I've been hearing for the past couple of nights.

"No, I don't whistle. Why?"

"Someone's whistling near my home at night. He keeps waking me up."

Peter frowns. "At night? What time?"

"I don't know. Two, three, sometimes four."

"On Maple Street? Strange. I pass by at least once a night, and I've never heard any whistling." He regards me seriously. "I don't like this. How many times have you heard it?"

"Almost every night. Maybe it's one of the other security guys?"

"We don't whistle when we're patrolling at night." He shakes his head. "Look, if you keep hearing those whistles late at night, someone might be trying to harass someone on your street, maybe even… Write down my phone number. If you hear that whistle again, call me. I'll be right over."

I pull out my phone, and he dictates his number.

"What's your last name?" I ask, saving his number.

"Just write down Peter from the security firm."

"Okay, thanks," I say, annoyed. What difference would it make to give me his last name? I shove my phone back inside my bag. "Have a nice day."

"You too." He nods. "Bye."

I walk on home. Deep down, I'm hoping that tonight the whistling will recur.

CHAPTER ELEVEN

Darkness. It was foolish, walking home so late. I should have asked someone for a ride. I walk quickly, the sound of my footsteps echoing in the eerily silent street. Hands in my pockets, it's so cold I can see my breath. Strange, I'm cold, and yet feel hot as well.

Someone behind me is walking and whistling. He whistles a strange tune, familiar, I feel like I've heard it before, but perhaps it's just my imagination. He seems to be getting closer, and fear engulfs me. He's following me, I'm sure of that, I have to get away from him. I hasten my steps, my breath quickening. The tune is getting louder, closer, and the tone becomes jarring, seemingly cruel. I mustn't run. If I run, he'll chase me. There is nothing to be afraid of, it's just some guy walking down the street, same as me. Walking faster and faster.

A dog barks in the darkness, my heart leaps, and I start running. I care for nothing, only getting home matters. The whistling stops, but I hear his footsteps as he starts running as well. He is definitely getting closer. He mustn't catch me, he mustn't… My ankle twists and I cry in pain and fear. A hand grabs my hair pulling me back, and a hoarse whisper in my ear. "Don't cry sweetheart… We are together at last."

I wake up, tears in my eyes. This was the worst nightmare so far, and that whistle, has it entered my dreams now?

The window is open, letting air into my room. Outside, I hear the familiar tune. It sends chills down my spine. I remember my dream, thinking that perhaps the person outside my window is somehow chasing me as well. I recall what Shane said and Peter hinted, someone could be trying to harass me, and a thought suddenly intrudes. Perhaps he doesn't want to harass me; perhaps he wants to catch me?

I nearly fall as I leap out of bed and turn on the light. I grab my phone and shakily call "Peter – security firm."

"Hello?" Peter's reassuring voice answers almost immediately.

"Hello, Peter? It's Amy." I try to control my voice. "The whistling outside. There's a... He is whistling outside." I peer outside the window carefully. I can't see anyone there.

"I'm on my way," he says and hangs up.

He's on his way. On his way is not good enough. Who knows how long it'll take? The person whistling is out there right now! I leave my room and do something that I haven't done since I was a little girl. I go to the door of my parents' bedroom and knock.

"What is it?" I hear Dad's drowsy voice.

"Can I come in?" I ask, practically begging.

"Sure, honey. Come right in."

I open the door. Dad turns on his bed lamp and looks at me sleepily. Mom's still sleeping. Mom doesn't wake up easily.

"What is it, Amy?" he says, concerned. "Are you all right?"

"Yes... no. There's that whistling outside again, and it's scaring me."

"What whistling?"

I become silent. In Dad and Mom's bedroom I can't hear the whistling, but their window faces the other side of the house.

"You've never heard whistling at night?"

"No. What kind of whistling?"

"Can you come with me to my room for a second?"

He gets up and follows me. When I was little, after my Grandmother died, I used to have bad dreams almost every night. Every time that would happen, it was always Dad who would come. He would be at my bedside within seconds after I would scream. He would hug me, and sometimes sleep in my room to calm me down. I always knew that if I had monsters in my closet, or under my bed, Dad would be the one to call.

I lead him to my room, and motion to him to be silent and listen. There's no sound.

Of course. Of course there isn't any whistling. I should have known.

"I think you just had a bad dream," Dad says, putting a reassuring hand on my shoulder. My phone rings, and he looks at me in surprise. "Who's calling you at this hour?"

I answer the phone. "Hello?"

"Amy? It's Peter. I'm standing next to your house, and there's no one here. I can't hear any whistling."

"And you didn't see anyone on the street?" I almost scream in frustration. Who is this mysterious whistler? Why is he harassing me?

"The whole street is completely silent. Are you sure you've heard whistling? It's just… there's nothing here."

"I guess it was just a dream," I say helplessly. "Never mind. Thanks, Peter."

I hang up. My father is scrutinizing me, his arms folded, his forehead furrowed. "Who was that?"

"The security guy. I called him when I heard the whistling."

"How did you have his phone number? Since when are you calling a security guy when you have a bad dream? Why didn't you come straight to me?"

Many questions and I have no answers. Damage control.

"I don't know. I was very scared." My voice is trembling, some tears. Good.

"Okay, okay," Dad says quickly. He can never handle my crying. "I understand, honey. Don't worry, it was just a bad dream. Come on, get back to bed."

I lay down, sniffing. Dad tucks me in, as if I was six years old again. He kisses me on my forehead.

"Should I turn off the light?" he asks, pausing in the doorway.

"No," I answer. "Please leave it on."

CHAPTER TWELVE

I meet Coral near social studies class. Today she's wearing a grey shirt with a worn out pattern, jeans which have seen better days, and sneakers. I really need to take this girl shopping someday. Nevertheless, fashion catastrophe or not, she is happy to talk to me, and that feels good.

"Coral, let's go for a walk."

Coral stares at me in shock. She looks as if I just asked her to dance nude with me in the schoolyard.

"What do you mean? We have a class now."

"Yes. We both have social studies. Let's skip it."

"But... She might teach something important."

"Something important? In social studies? Like what?"

"I don't know. Something about... pilgrims?"

"I can't be in social studies class right now. I'm too tired. Let's skip it."

"But... What if they call my parents?"

"Just tell them that the guidance counselor told you to help another student with their class work, and didn't tell your teacher." I look at her frustrated. Hasn't she ever done this before?

"I... Tell them... But... They might talk to the guidance counselor and... and..."

I sigh. "There's no reason they'd talk to the guidance counselor. Okay, listen." I shift the bag on my back. "I'm going. You coming?"

She looks distraught. "Maybe... some other time."

"Fantastic," I say tiredly. "Another time, then."

I walk away. "Amy!" she says.

"What?"

"What should I do when she takes attendance? What should I tell her?"

"You don't have to tell her anything. Don't worry about it." I ignore her unhappy face and leave. Back in LA, I never had any problem convincing Nicole to split. Nicole was my splitting partner. I spot Shane down the hall. Yesterday I was annoyed by his weird gallantry. Today it seems a little less weird. And I need to talk to a friend. Any friend.

"Shane!"

"Hey, how are you?" He smiles.

"Feel like skipping whatever class you're about to have?"

"Sure." He nods. "Let's go out to the football field."

"Great, the football field," I say, relieved to have someone whom I can easily convince to skip class with me.

We sit down outside on the lawn, in the shade of a small tree. Shane pulls out his camera and begins inspecting it.

"Only in Narrowdale is there a street which cats never enter," he says.

I lift an eyebrow. He shoots an innocent look my way and returns to tinkering with his irritating camera.

"Only in Narrowdale...," I say, trying to think of something. "Only in Narrowdale do aliens kidnap people and... uh... eat them."

"Come on." He laughs. "You're not even trying. Aliens? Seriously? I am almost sure that no one has ever been kidnapped here by an alien."

"I'm sure there's no street here which cats won't enter."

"Really?"

I stay silent.

Shane turns on his camera and aims it at me. "Only in Narrowdale lives a woman with more than two hundred hamsters in her basement."

"You're just making this up."

"Why should I?" he grins. "She gives each one a name. And at night she plots with them how to murder her ex-husband."

"This game is idiotic."

"So what? It passes the time."

"True."

"Your turn."

"Only in Narrowdale… Do you have to film me?"

He turns off the camera.

"Thanks. Only in Narrowdale does someone walk around at night, whistling a tune that only I can hear."

Shane frowns and says nothing.

"Look, I…"

"I made you uncomfortable yesterday, didn't I?" he says.

I shrug. "Yeah, I guess."

"Sorry. I'm a bit clumsy with people, as you can probably tell." He smiles, embarrassed. "I just thought you might appreciate the help."

I look at him, blushing. He seems really earnest. I realize I've judged him without giving him a chance. And frankly, I need all the help I can get.

"Shane… I actually do appreciate it. Um… if I hear the whistling tonight, can I call you?"

"Sure." He perks up.

"And you'll come by?"

"No problem."

"But… I don't want you walking around my house at night alone. I'll come out and we'll check it out together."

"Are you sure? Wouldn't you rather let me check it out on my own?"

"No. If it's nothing, I want to see it's nothing."

"And if it's something?"

"If it's something, two are better than one."

Shane nods.

"Only in Narrowdale," I start to say, but the school bell interrupts me.

"Let's skip the next class as well," I suggest, but Shane politely refuses.

"Coward," I mumble and go to English class. I sit down next to Coral, yawning.

"I wrote everything down, so you can copy my notes."

"You're the best." I yawn.

"And I can explain anything you don't understand."

"Awesome."

"But she took attendance." She looks at me sadly. She probably thinks I'm going to jail, and that she might never see me again.

"Coral, that's fine, don't worry about it."

"Hey, Amy," someone says behind me. I turn around. It's Jasmine. What does she want? She has a small, chilly smile.

"Yeah?"

"I heard you called the security guy in the middle of the night, to come and rescue you."

I can feel myself blush in humiliation. How could she have heard about it? And so soon?

"What's the matter?" asked Carley, sitting next to her. "Felt lonely?"

I stare at them both in stunned silence. They smile at me, evil smiles, showing perfect white teeth. What do they want from me? I open my mouth to lash out, then close it. I have nothing to say. They snigger and I turn back and cover my face with my hands. I hate this place.

"What are they talking about?" asks Coral. "Amy?"

I stay silent.

Mrs. Parker, the English teacher, storms in and starts yelling randomly. "Linda! The lesson's started! Sit down! Paul, silence! Mark, silence! Do I have to ask each and every one of you personally?"

I don't understand what the fuss is about. It wouldn't hurt if once in a while a teacher would ask for silence from each and every one of us personally. It's polite, it's nice, and it would make us feel special. Mrs. Parker snatches a marker and start writing furiously on the whiteboard. After two letters, the marker slips from her hand and drops on the floor.

"Silence!" she roars. No one was talking. Coral and I exchange petrified glances. What's with this insane teacher?

Mrs. Parker takes a different marker and starts writing down several words. It's all so blurry, and I'm so tired…

"Monologue," says Mrs. Parker, pointing at the first word. "Who can define the word monologue?"

Someone raises his hand. He starts talking, and my eyes slowly shut. There's no point being in the class, I really don't know why I even came here. Mrs. Parker voice drones in my ears.

"Kidnapping," she says. "Define kidnapping."

No one answers.

"For example," says Mrs. Parker. "While walking down the street, she was kidnapped by a stranger. Anyone?"

I get up and walk out of class. Mrs. Parker doesn't even notice. "Fine. Let's try a different word," she carries on. "Stalking."

I walk down the school halls. Silence surrounds me. The students are all in class and the school looks practically abandoned. I approach one of the classrooms, peek through a crack in the door. The room is empty, dark. I open the door and walk in.

Darkness, I can't see a thing. I can't move, can't shout. Something fills my mouth, blocking it. I try to spit it out, but I can't. He's here, I know he's here, I can hear him breathe. I struggle, my hands tied. Something's trickling down my cheek. Something warm. If only there was some light here… My head hurts. I have to get out of here. Someone will come and rescue me. He's here. He starts whistling, it's that tune again. He approaches me, I can feel him inches from my face, he stops whistling, and whispers hoarsely, "Don't worry, sweetheart, I'm here…"

"Amy!"

I open my eyes and scream. Everyone is looking at me. Some of the students are laughing. Did I fall asleep during class? How did that happen? Mrs. Parker stares at me, livid.

"What was that?" she starts shrieking. "Where do you think you are? Do you think this is the–"

I don't stay around to hear what this is. I grab my bag, and dash out of class.

CHAPTER THIRTEEN

Any hope I had of making a good impression has been completely lost. I will forever be remembered as the girl who fell asleep in class and woke up screaming. These are things that people never forget.

I'm home by twelve thirty. No one is in and the door's locked. I rummage through my bag, and for one terrible moment I think I have no key, but I finally find it, hidden in the corner. I unlock the door and go straight to the bathroom. I wash my face and breathe deeply, trying to calm down.

I need to talk to someone, but all my friends are in class. I try to reach out anyway, sending messages to all of them. Jennifer Williams answers me with a rebuking message – "Why are you not in class?"

I scroll through all my contacts twice. I can't call Mom and Dad. They'll ask why I'm not in school, and I'll just get in trouble. Anthony doesn't answer his phone, as always. Who can I call? The cable support service? The airline tickets hotline?

My finger wavers next to Peter's contact. I really want to hear his voice.

I wait for several seconds, and he answers. "Hello?" He sounds very sleepy.

"Peter?"

"Who's that?" I woke him up. Why's he sleeping? It's the middle of the day... Oh, god, I'm such an idiot! He had a night shift! I should know that, I called him at night...

"It's Amy. Never mind, I'm sorry I woke you up."

"Amy?" he asks confused. "Is everything okay?"

"Yes I just… I wanted to apologize about last night."

"You have nothing to apologize for," he mumbles drowsily. "Glad to help. But I would like to go back to sleep, please."

"Sure, bye!" I hang up, cursing myself. Now he'll think I'm some sort of stalker or something.

I have to find some way to keep myself busy. I turn on the television, flip the channels for five minutes. I turn off the television. I go to my room, turn on my computer, and check the comments on my blog. No new comments. I go back down to the living room, turn around, return to my room, and search for a book to read, but nothing seems attractive. I walk to the kitchen, pour myself some cold water, drink one sip, put the glass in the sink. Open the fridge, close the fridge, stare at the fridge door. I organize the magnets on the fridge in the shape of a circle, then I organize them in the shape of a square. Mom walks in.

"Amy? What are you doing home?" Mom looks at me with surprise.

"School ended early today. There was a sick… um… teacher."

"Okay." It was actually a long "okay" with a rising intonation, ending with a note of a query. More like "Oookaaay…?" along with one raised eyebrow. I never cease to be amazed by the amount of significance that Mom can give to a simple word.

"Come on. I need some help with the groceries," she says.

I help Mom haul the shopping bags from the car into the kitchen. I start putting away the cans. I like cans. Corn, beans, peas.

Mom sighs.

"Is everything all right?" I ask.

"We didn't get yogurt," she answers. I don't know who "we" is exactly. I'm certainly not a part of this "we," since I didn't go shopping; only Mom did.

Sugar. Where does the sugar go in this place?

"Don't you have homework?" Mom asks.

"No, I have nothing."

"I see," she says. In fact, she says "I *see*" emphasizing the "see," as if the fact that I have no homework proves some complex theory that she built, and she is about to publish an important article on the subject.

I choose a random cupboard and shove the sugar inside. Slowly but surely the shopping bags become empty.

"Amy, you seem a little tired," Mom notes, watching me with a worried expression. "Perhaps you should lie down a little."

Rest. Sleep. Dream.

"No, I'm fine," I say. "I think I'll go take a shower."

There's a knock on the door. It's the air conditioning technician again. He came to fix the noise that the air conditioning is making. I walk away to the shower.

When I'm leaving the bathroom, the technician is banging something with a hammer. What's a hammer got to do with fixing the air conditioning? Every bang feels as if it's landing on my skull.

My phone rings. It's Coral.

"Hey."

"Amy! Is everything all right?"

"Yeah... super."

"Super? What happened in class today? Mrs. Parker couldn't teach a thing after you left. She simply couldn't make anyone calm down! They were all talking about you..."

"I've always wanted to be famous," I say miserably. Everyone was talking about me. They'll never forget this. Even when I'm eighty-four, losing my teeth, I'll still be the one who seventy years ago fell asleep in class and woke up screaming.

"But what happened?" Coral sounds worried. "Why–"

"I had a bad dream."

"In class?"

"Yeah, I guess I just fell asleep."

"Amy, you have to try and sleep more. You know, if you don't get enough sleep, your DNA starts to unravel."

"Seriously?" I rub my eyes. "What does that even mean?"

"I don't know, but I read it somewhere."

"Well, I can't really do anything about that," I sigh. "I really can't sleep, Coral. I just can't. But I appreciate your concern. Anyway, listen, the air conditioning guy is here. He is banging on something, and I can hardly hear a word you're saying. Let's talk later, okay?"

"Okay. Amy…"

"What?"

"I hope you feel better," she says hesitantly. Coral thinks that I am sick. She might be right. Hopefully I really will start feeling better. I hang up.

The hammering gets stronger. Each thump feels as if it is intended to break my brain into tiny pieces.

When will this day finally end?

CHAPTER FOURTEEN

Something warm and sticky is running down my cheek, but I can't wipe it. I can't move my hands, and once more, I hear the whistling. I try to talk, but my mouth seems to be blocked. Where am I? Why is it so dark? The liquid on my cheek drips on the floor. Water? Another drop trickles down and drops, making a familiar dripping sound. The whistling becomes louder, a door opens. A dark silhouette is standing in the doorway, and the light behind it hurts my eyes. I avert my face and look downwards, towards a small puddle of water. No, not water. Blood.

My eyes open and I'm staring at my room's ceiling, shivering. The nightmares are not letting up. If this goes on, I'll ask Mom to send me to therapy. My body is tired, but my brain won't let it go back to sleep. In sleep, the darkness awaits.

The whistling. I can still hear the whistling. Of course, this was not actually part of my dream, just something that intertwined with it. Tonight this ends. I grab my phone and call Shane.

"Amy?" he answers, sounding completely awake. I glance at my alarm clock. It's a quarter past one.

"Are you awake?" I ask, stupidly.

"Yes. Do you need me to come over?"

I take a deep breath. After this there is no going back. Then again, I guess there is no going back after calling him in the middle of the night.

"Yes. I live on Maple Street."

"I know, you told me."

"Number thirteen. It's the one next to the house with the really ugly veranda."

"I'm on my way."

"Don't knock on the door, and try to be silent. Call me once you're here."

He hangs up. My heart is pumping. I peek out the window and see no one. I put on a pair of pants and a shirt and wait. The whistling doesn't stop, the tune strange and disturbing, making me recall images from my dreams. I put my phone on vibrate. The waiting is nerve-racking. I wonder if Peter is patrolling tonight. My fingers drum on the side of my bed nervously. The whistling doesn't fade, doesn't stop, the same eerie tune over and over. I feel like I've been waiting for hours, but the clock says it's only been fifteen minutes.

My phone vibrates.

"I'm outside," says Shane when I answer.

"Can you hear it?" I ask, and I suddenly know that he'll say, "Hear what? Whistling? What whistling?" And then I'll know for sure that something really bad happened to me, that I've lost my mind, that…

"I can hear it."

I breathe out in relief. I'm not crazy. Someone is out there, and I need to confront him.

I put on my shoes and walk out.

CHAPTER FIFTEEN

As I open the front door, I can hear the whistling more clearly. My heart beats faster as I stand in the doorway, my hand still holding the door handle. This is much more frightening than I thought it would be. It's one thing to hear someone creepy whistling outside my window. It's a completely different thing to hear him as I'm standing outside, nothing but space between us. I suddenly feel vulnerable and helpless. What was I thinking? What did I plan to do if I caught up to this guy? Whimper at him? Because this is pretty much what I can do right now, and I don't think it will scare him off. What if he's some sort of pervert, or… or…

Or a stranger, chasing you on the street, grabbing your hair, whispering in your ear…

I shake my head. I should call Shane, tell him to check it out on his own. My hand creeps towards my pocket, going for the phone, and then Shane's head pops above the fence.

"Hey," he whispers. "Coming?"

And I know I can't back out. Partly because the thought of telling Shane that I'm too scared makes me want to throw up. Partly because I really do want to see the person whistling. He's not the boogeyman. He's just some creepy guy, whistling in the street in the middle of the night.

I walk outside. Shane is holding his video camera, and points it at me as I come near him.

"Why are you filming?" I ask, irritated.

"Would you rather I didn't?"

I open my mouth to tell him this is serious business, that this is no time to work on his reality show… and then I pause. This might be a good idea. If this really is some creepy guy, it might be smart to have him on film. I could show the film to Mom and Dad or to Peter, have them take care of the problem.

"No. That's actually a good idea. Film it, but send me the video afterwards."

"Yeah, okay."

I look around and try to figure out where the whistling is actually coming from. "I think it's coming from there."

I start walking and Shane follows, pointing the camera at me, then at the street. The whistling sound becomes louder as we get closer… but then it starts to fade. I can still hear it, but it feels as if whoever is whistling is walking away.

"I think it's fading," I whisper. "He's getting away. Maybe he heard us."

"I'm not sure," Shane answers. "Maybe, but it doesn't sound too far. I think it's coming from the street over there." He points his camera at a small street intersecting with mine.

"All right, let's go," I say, trying to sound determined. Frankly, if the whistling stopped right now, I would probably be relieved.

We walk down the street, our footsteps echoing in the darkness. He can probably hear us. There is no other sound except for our steps and his whistling. Nevertheless, as we walk down the street Shane pointed us to, the shrill tune becomes louder.

"It sounds really close," Shane whispers. "Where is he?"

I don't know. The street seems empty as the whistling becomes louder and louder. We've stopped walking, but it's still getting closer. He's so close! I frantically look around at the shadows, the trees, the bushes. A creepy image flashes through my head, someone crawling through a bush, whistling, his eyes shining in malice…

Don't worry, sweetheart, I'm here…

"Where is he?" Shane shouts, panicking.

The tune is incredibly loud. No one can whistle that loud. It sounds like he's whistling into my ear, yet there's no one here! I'm whirling around, breathing hard, gasping, half sobbing.

"I don't know!" I shout back. "I can't see him!"

He's here! Above us, below us, behind us, but there's no one. No one at all, just a loud, insane, shrill tune, screeching in my ear over and over and over and...

It stops.

I let out a long breath.

"Okay, what–"

A terrible scream interrupts me. It sounds like someone who's frightened beyond sense, screaming helplessly, terror, pain and helplessness mingling into one long wail.

"Shane!" I sob, grasping his hand.

"Let's get out of here!" He pulls me away. We run back down the street, the scream still echoing in my ears. I run as fast as I can, Shane pulling me forward, not letting go. The darkness feels as if it is closing around us, and I know for a certainty that whoever was whistling in the street is behind us, closing in, getting closer and closer and closer...

A large shadow looms ahead. I let out a frightened scream.

"Amy?"

A flashlight turns on, and behind its blinding beam of light I glimpse the outline of a familiar face.

"Peter!"

CHAPTER SIXTEEN

"Amy!" Peter is shouting. "What happened? Are you all right?"

"Peter, you have to go there!" I'm hysterical, on the verge of crying. "You have to!"

"What do you mean? Go where? What are you talking about?" Peter stares at both of us. "What are you doing outside this late?"

"That scream." Shane is breathing hard. "Someone needs help."

"A woman," I say. "It's a woman who needs help. Come on, Peter!" I look at him in frustration. "Go check it out!"

"What scream?" asks Peter. "Where did it come from? I didn't hear anything."

"I don't believe it! You didn't hear it? The whole town probably heard it. Over there! The scream came from over there!" I point back to where we came from.

Peter seems troubled. He obviously doesn't want to leave us alone, but he doesn't want to take us somewhere that might be dangerous.

"Stay here," he finally says. "Don't go anywhere!"

We wait obediently as he runs towards the street we came from.

"Amy?" says Shane. "What was that?"

"I don't know." I am shivering.

"That whistling sounded as if it was all around us. But there was no one there."

"I know."

"And that scream."

"I know."

"What do you think that was?"

I don't answer. I don't know what that was. I don't know what's happening to my life.

"Is your camera still on?" I ask.

"No," he answers. "I turned it off when the security guy turned up."

"His name is Peter. You filmed everything else?"

He nods.

"Can you send it to me when you get home?"

"Sure, no problem. Why?"

"Because I want to see what happened."

Peter returns. "I found nothing. The street is totally quiet. There was no one there. Can you tell me what you heard? And what you were doing outside?"

"We heard whistling...," starts Shane.

"It wasn't clear where it came from."

"...It felt like it was right on top of us..."

"Even around us."

"Someone screamed..."

"Perhaps the person who was whistling..."

Peter lifts his hand, and we both quiet down.

"Okay, I didn't understand one bit," he says. "I'll alert the police, and start patrolling the entire area thoroughly. I want you both to go straight home. I won't have you walking around by yourselves in the middle of the night." He stares at us severely. "Do I need to walk you home?"

"I can walk myself," Shane says quickly.

"I... I'd appreciate it if you walked me home," I say.

"I can—" Shane starts to say, but Peter interrupts him. "I want you to go back home. I'll walk Amy."

Shane shrugs, glances at me, and walks away.

"All right." Peter nods my way. "Let's go."

We walk silently towards my house.

"You won't say anything to my parents, right?" I say.

He hesitates. "No, but you're going to tell them all about it, okay?"

"Sure!" I instantly lie. "First thing in the morning."

"Good." We reach my house. "Okay. I hope the rest of your night is peaceful. And Amy…"

"Yes?"

"I don't want to see you in the streets in the middle of the night again. Young girls shouldn't be outside this late."

I swallow my tears. "Fine. Thanks," I say, and walk inside.

CHAPTER SEVENTEEN

"Amy? Hey, it's Peter."

"Hey," I say tiredly, lying on my bed, the phone pressed against my ear. Sunlight shines through the window.

"Amy, are you… all right?"

"I'm a bit sick."

"Really? Listen, I did a thorough search last night, and found nothing. I didn't hear anything unusual either."

"Great, that's good to know."

"What were you and your boyfriend doing outside in the middle of the night?"

"He's not my boyfriend."

"Yeah, okay, but what–"

"Peter, do you sometimes think that Narrowdale is a strange place?"

Small pause. "Are you talking about all those funny stories people tell?"

"What funny stories?"

"Those ridiculous urban legends. Strange voices in weird places, red eyes appearing in the dark… You know, nonsense."

"I haven't heard any stories," I lie. Where have we moved? What was wrong with LA? "Are you sure it's all nonsense?"

"Things always have an explanation. Every time I check up on something like that, it turns out that the strange sound is a cat that got stuck in the shed, or that the huge serpent was actually a lifelike statue. Look, don't believe a word people say. Narrowdale is just like any other place."

"Really?"

"I swear."

I think about it. Could all my experiences have an everyday explanation? The scream, the whistling, the dreams? I guess some of it can be easily explained. Maybe Narrowdale *is* just like any other place. Except it isn't. It really isn't. But how can I make Peter realize that?

I sit up. "Edgar," I say.

"Sorry?"

"That guy, Edgar? The homeless guy?"

"What about him?"

"He isn't... usual. He knows things."

"Edgar? He's just a bit crazy. Harmless, but..."

"What did Edgar tell you when you tried to get him to leave the shopping mall?"

"What?"

"You told me that you tried to get him to leave the shopping mall once. What did he tell you when you did that?"

"What difference does it make? What were you doing outside last night?"

"I'll tell you if you tell me."

There's a moment of silence. Peter seems to be fond of silence. "Okay, look, he said he knows when I'm going to die. He asked if I wanted to know the date."

My skin crawls. "Does that sound normal to you?" I ask hysterically. "Does that sound like something that someone might say anywhere?"

"Come on! It was just talk. The guy doesn't know what he's saying. One minute he's blathering about spirits and talking animals, the next he's talking about something he ate yesterday. Now tell me, what were you and your boyfr... I mean, friend, doing outside in the middle of the night?"

"We were trying to find the guy whistling in my street."

"Why didn't you call me?"

"I didn't feel like it."

"You should call me when something like that happens."

"Well, what do I know? I'm just a little girl."

"You're not a little girl. You're very mature."

"That's not what you said last night!"

"What? I just said I don't want to see you outside in the middle of the night!"

"Yeah, because I'm a little girl." That's not a tear. Well, fine, it is a tear, but I've got something in my eye.

"No! I just don't want you chasing strange people at night! It could be dangerous!" He sounds worried. "Amy, please let me do my job and keep you safe."

He wants to keep me safe. My face feels hot. "Fine. Did you find out who screamed last night?"

"I told you; I heard nothing. The police came around this morning and we questioned all the residents in the street. No one heard anything."

"Okay."

"Perhaps there was no scream," he suggests. "I bet it was a cat."

"Right. A cat."

"You know how they sound when they're mating."

"Yeah. Mating."

"Hey, listen, I hope you feel better. I have to go."

"Okay. Thanks."

http://amy.strangerealm.com/whistle.html

CHAPTER EIGHTEEN

The air conditioning guy is here again, and I leave home to escape the noise. Why does he need a drill to fix an air conditioner?

The sun outside is scorching hot as usual, no way to escape its glare.

"Good morning."

I whirl in fright. A bit nervous, aren't you, Amy? It's just Alex, the neighbor.

"Good morning." I smile shakily. He is standing in his front yard with his dog, looking at me. He's wearing the same jeans that he's always wearing, and a horrid striped shirt that no one in their right mind would even buy, never mind wear.

"Aren't you going to school today?"

"I'm sick," I answer. "How's your dog?"

"Moka."

"Sorry?"

"Moka. Her name is Moka. She's doing great. Your mother told me that she was barking during the night, so now she sleeps inside. She's very happy with this new arrangement." He smiles a thin smile. "And you? Are you sleeping better now that Moka doesn't wake you up?"

"Oh, definitely. Much better. I sleep like a baby."

Oh?" he raises his eyebrow. "The babies I know wake up at least four times a night. Shouldn't you be in bed if you're sick?"

"Someone's fixing our air conditioner, and he's making a lot of noise."

"Noise, huh? That's a problem. I heard some noise last night."

"Really?" I play innocent. "What noise?"

"A noise of children looking for things that shouldn't be found," he replies heavily. "Did you hear something like that?"

"I... I have to go inside." I turn around and open our front door.

"There are dangerous things out here at night, girl," he mutters. "You should take care not to meet one of them."

I hurry inside and slam the door behind me. I have to talk to Shane. I quickly text him to call me when he can. A minute later I text Coral as well.

I pace back and forth in the living room, biting my nails. What did Alex mean? It definitely sounded like a threat. Could he be the one who was whistling outside? Impossible. The whistling was right in front of us, and we didn't see him. Alex is a big guy. We would have noticed him. Besides, that scream... It couldn't have been him. Perhaps I should talk to Mom and Dad? What would they say if I told them? Dad might go and have a chat with Alex. Is that a good idea? Alex will tell them that their daughter went out in the middle of the night with a boy, that he merely told her that she should be careful. What is the punishment for going out in the middle of the night with a boy from school to chase mysterious whistling? One week without a cell phone? Two weeks with no Internet? Two months without allowance?

"Kid, you're making me dizzy," remarks the air conditioning guy. "You've been walking around in circles for the past twenty minutes. At least change your direction once in a while."

I stare at him coldly. "Say, how long till the air conditioning works? This heat is unbearable."

He grins. "In a couple of hours, God willing."

God willing? God is helping him to fix the air conditioning? I go to my room and sit in front of my laptop. Seven comments on the last blog post I made, in which I wrote about our nightly adventure. I read the comments irritably, tapping on my desk. My phone blips - a new message from Shane. It's the video from last night. I watch the video. As it progresses I can feel myself tense. When the scream sounds, I jump in my chair and pause the video. Rewind a bit and play. Scream. Rewind and play. Scream. Rewind...

A knock on the door. "Is everything okay?" It's the technician.

"Everything's great," I answer. "I'm just screaming here by myself because I'm so hot."

I can hear him walking away. I plug in my earphones and carry on watching the video repeatedly, trying to figure out what happened yesterday...

My phone rings.

"Hi, Amy?"

"Shane! Are you at school?" I rewind the video again; watch the last couple of seconds, the voice muted.

"No, I stayed home."

"Oh? What did you tell your parents?"

"Nothing, they aren't home. They go out very early in the morning."

"Oh. Listen, you're not going to believe what happened..."

"I was there, remember? I just sent you the video–"

"I'm not talking about that! My neighbor talked to me this morning. He said that he heard us going out last night, and that I should watch myself because there are dangerous things outside or something."

"Okay, I think he might be right."

"He said it in a threatening way."

"Yeah? More threatening than a whistle without a person? Or a terrible scream in the middle of the street? Amy, we should call the cops."

"And tell them what? Peter already reported the scream. They've asked around and found nothing. Anyway, I don't want the cops to talk to my parents."

"Fine, fine." He sounds distressed. "So what do you want to do?"

"What do you think happened last night?" I ask.

"I... I'm not sure. That shrieking whistle was right on top of us and we saw no one. Could the person whistling be hiding? And that scream, a horrible scream, like an animal–"

"Not an animal," I interrupt. "It was a woman screaming."

"I don't think so. It sounded–"

"I've listened to this scream at least a dozen times." In fact it was more like two dozen, but I didn't want to sound obsessive. "I'm telling you, it was a woman's scream. I'm positive."

"So what happened to her? Where is she? That security guy didn't seem as if he was going to look for her. He was too busy walking you home."

"He never heard the scream, or the whistle. Anyway, he did check it out later."

Shane becomes silent, and so do I.

"Maybe we should let it go," suggests Shane hesitantly. "Perhaps your neighbor is right."

"I can't." I frown. "I haven't been sleeping for more than a week. If this keeps on, I'll lose my mind. I have to understand what's going on."

"Amy, what do you want to do?"

"Do you feel like checking out that place again?" I ask. "You know, where we heard the scream."

"Sure, there's nothing I'd rather do," he sighs. "Fine, I'll be at your place in half an hour."

CHAPTER NINETEEN

"Right," says Shane. "In daylight, this street looks much less spooky."

I have to agree. I scan the area, trying to figure out where the scream came from last night. Nothing. It just doesn't make any sense.

"Where do you think the scream came from?"

Shane shrugs.

My phone rings. It's Nicole. I ignore it.

I scrutinize the street thoroughly. What am I looking for? Shane starts whistling, and suddenly I feel dizzy. The answer is right there... What is it? I turn to face Shane.

"There's something... I'm having déjà vu," I say. "I feel like I've been here before."

"You were here last night," he points out.

"No. Before that." I start walking down the street. "Shane," I say without turning, "can you whistle again? You know, the tune from last night."

He starts whistling. I'm walking...

Walking down the silent street in the middle of the night. Something's wrong with the streetlights, they're not working, and the darkness surrounds me. I should have asked for a ride. I shove my hands down in my coat pockets, shivering. It's cold tonight, very cold. My footsteps tap on the sidewalk, their sound echoing strangely. Nothing moves, but I feel as if someone is watching me. It must be my imagination. Who would walk out here so late at night? I start walking faster, wanting to get home already. I can hear something behind me. Another person, another late walker. He begins whistling. His whistle is unpleasant, penetrating. I want to get away from him. I'll be home soon. The whistling is getting louder; he's getting nearer. It's nothing. I start running, I have to get home. The whistling stops, I hear him running after me. He's gaining! The heel of my shoe twists and I trip. He grabs my hair and whispers… I scream…

I struggle frantically with my captor, swinging my elbow backwards, feeling it sink in the attacker's stomach, hearing him gasp. He lets go and I whirl around…

Shane is lying on the sidewalk, trying to breathe.

"Shane!" I call out in fright. "Are you okay?"

"Sure," he wheezes. "I'm great. I love getting sucker-punched." I help him get up.

"I'm s-sorry," I stutter. "You scared me, I thought you were…"

What? What was I thinking? What just happened? It was dark, and cold. I look around unbelievingly, feeling the sun's scorching light on my face. My dream trickled into reality. It was… I look around me and something finally connects. This street is the same street that I've been dreaming of. This is the street where I run away from the person who's chasing me, who catches me and whispers that we're finally together.

"Why did you run?" asks Shane, breathing hard. "The way that you ran and screamed… is everything okay? Did a bee sting you or something?"

"No, not a bee. I think I might be going insane." I look at him, scared. "I keep having dreams about this street. The dreams I told you about. Someone is chasing me. He grabs my hair."

"Okay." He nods. "So what do you think that means?"

"Shane, I've never been to this street until last night. How could I have been dreaming about it for a whole week?"

"It could be a similar street. All streets here look the same."

"No!" I shout at him. "Not similar! The bus stop here! The trash can over there! The white fence on the other side! Everything exactly like my dream! Here, next to this fire hydrant is where he catches me!"

"Amy," he raises his hands, trying to calm me down, his eyes darting around. "Relax. You've probably seen this street before."

I burst out laughing hysterically. "Only in Narrowdale… Only in Narrowdale is there whistling with no one to whistle, screaming that some hear and some don't, dreams that come back to haunt you every night…" I stop laughing and breathe hard.

"Come on," he says. "Let's go to your place."

"No." I sniff. "The air conditioning guy is over there. I can't stand the noise anymore. Can we go to your place?"

"Sure," he nods. "Let's go to my place then. I think you need to have a soda and rest a little."

CHAPTER TWENTY

Shane's home is ten minutes away. As we walk inside I take a look around me. It's a living room. I've seen one of those before.

Shane leads me to his room. A bed, bookshelves containing about a million books, a desk with a computer, a video camera, and a digital pocket camera. Everything is incredibly tidy. Nothing is tossed on the floor or on the desk. The sheet on the bed is stretched tight, the blanket folded at the bottom. If my Mom could see Shane's room, she'd replace me with him in an instant.

"Where do you keep your mess?" I ask.

"The room is tidy right now by accident," he says uncomfortably. "Sometimes this room is in complete chaos, believe me."

I'm sure. I bet sometimes there's a pencil just sitting there on the desk.

"Can I get you something to drink?"

"I don't know. Is there anything tasty?" I regret my stupid question immediately. How could he possibly know what I like?

"There's Coke."

"Coke is fine."

"Coke it is." He leaves the room.

I overcome my immediate urge to open closets and drawers, being the good girl that I am. I examine the books in his library. They all have names like *"Sword of Truth"* or *"Dragon's Fire."* This irritates me incredibly, though I'm unsure why. I pace around the room, sit down on the bed, get up immediately, straighten the crease I've made on the meticulous order of the sheets, return to scrutinizing the library, start to contemplate opening a drawer after all. My phone rings. It's Coral.

"Hey, Coral."

"Amy, is everything all right? I just got your message."

"That's fine."

"I turn my phone off in school, you know, so that it won't distract me."

"Sure, I get it."

"But… What did you want to talk about? Is everything okay?"

"Yes. No. I don't know."

Shane walks in with two glasses of Coke. I motion that I'm talking on the phone. He puts one glass on the desk and sits on the bed. I sit on the chair next to the desk.

"Why didn't you come to school today? Are you sick?" Coral asks.

"No. I… I had a rough night."

"What happened?"

"Coral, I'm sending you a video that Shane took last night. Watch it and then we'll talk, okay?"

"Okay, but what happened last night?"

"Coral, after you see the video."

"So you're sending it…"

"Right now."

"Okay. Bye."

"Bye." I hang up and start sending the message. Shane watches me quietly.

"Do you read only fantasy books?" I ask while texting.

"No," he answers. "I read other things as well."

I glance at his library. "Prove it."

"Drink up. It's hot outside." He sips. I do the same. I regret not asking for water, but asking for another glass seems stupid. I finally send the message.

"What do you want to do?" he asks.

"Sleep."

"I mean, what do you want to do with your dreams, and the whistling we heard, and the–"

"I don't know. I want it to stop. I want to sleep. I haven't slept for more than a week."

"Maybe you could consult with someone," he says carefully. "You know, a professional…" He stops and stares intently at his glass.

"You heard the whistling," I answer. "And the scream. Do you think a shrink can help me with that?"

"There must be a simple explanation, and your dreams don't have to be connected. You're just mixing up unrelated things. The whistling is just some weirdo walking outside your home at night. You just have to find out who it is and make him stop. The dreams are probably because of the heat and the stress of the new school."

"And what's your enlightening explanation to the scream we heard?"

"I don't know. Maybe it really was a cat. Or maybe someone in a house nearby was watching a horror movie and we heard his television."

I want to agree. If everything has a logical explanation, then my life will go back to normal. The air conditioner will start working, and I'll be able to sleep at night. Everyone in the new class will love me, and it will all work out.

My phone rings again. I expect it to be Coral, but it's Nicole again.

"Honey!!!" she screams in my ear. "You're so crazy! What kind of posts are you uploading to your blog? Jennifer nearly fainted!"

"Yeah, Nicole, I–"

"What the hell do you think you're doing, chasing strangers in the middle of the night?" asks Nicole. "Are you trying to get into trouble? Out of our sight for two seconds, and already messing around."

"I just wanted to tell that guy who's whistling outside my window to stop!"

"Honey, people get killed doing things like that. You have to be more careful. Listen, I think you need some time off. Do you want to come here for the weekend? You can sleep at my place."

"That sounds good," I answer, relieved. I don't have nightmares in LA. "I'll talk to my mom. And tell Jen that I'm okay. Really, she doesn't need to lose sleep over it or anything."

"Okay. Honey, you'll never believe what happened. You remember Jack, the guy I met when we went to the park that day? So get this—"

"Nicole, I'm kind of in the middle of something. I'll talk to you later. And I'm really looking forward to seeing you over the weekend."

"All right, all right," she says. "Talk to you later. Bye!"

I hang up and look at Shane. He's drinking his Coke, looking embarrassed.

"A friend from LA," I explain. "She wanted to know about the blog. I wrote about the fun night we had."

"Yeah, I got it."

"I'm going to LA for the weekend. Maybe I'll manage to sleep there."

Shane nods. "Sounds like a good plan."

"Yeah," I say. "Maybe that's all I need. A little bit of home."

"You know, Narrowdale's your home now."

I shut my eyes tiredly. This conversation is wearing me down.

"Nice cameras you have there," I say, changing the topic. "I thought you only filmed videos."

"No, I like to take photos as well," Shane answers. "Sometimes you can really capture the essence of a situation much better with photos."

"Nice. Do you have any photographs I can see?" I ask, interested.

He opens a drawer. Inside there's a large pile of albums. I notice some more drawers underneath the one opened and wonder if there are more albums in there as well. He lifts the topmost album from the drawer and hands it to me.

I turn to the first page. "Why do you print the pictures in black and white?" I ask, flipping the pages. Photographs of houses, of people, all in black and white.

"Not everything's black and white," he answers. "Just this last batch. I try different things. Here, check this one out, I took it just outside school last week."

"Cool," I say distractedly. Photographs are not my thing. I keep flipping the pages. A lot of photographs of the same house. It looks like any other house.

"What's up with this house?" I ask.

He shuffles in apparent discomfort. "I saw something in one of the windows in that house. I tried to take its picture."

"What was it?"

"Probably nothing," he answers. "I just thought… Sometimes I see things in town. Things that most people don't see. Know what I mean?"

I don't answer.

"This place," he waves his arms around him. "Strange things happen here. 'Only in Narrowdale' is not just a game, you know? It's part of living here. Some people see more, some less. I think some of them see nothing. My parents always act as if nothing's weird here. But I… I sometimes do see things."

"And what were you trying to photograph?"

"I was looking at this house, and through one of the windows… I thought I saw a tree."

"A tree inside the house?"

"Yeah."

"It was probably just a reflection, or just a large plant."

"No," he says. "There was no tree in the street. Only inside the house. A really tall tree, and kinda weird looking. I never saw a tree like that anywhere else. But I took a picture, and you can't see it. And when I came closer, I couldn't see it anymore."

A week ago I would have run away from here, screaming. But after the things that have happened to me in the past week…

My phone rings again, and I answer.

"Amy? What is that?" Coral sounds frightened.

"What is what?" I flip another page. Pictures of the moon. Two pages full of pictures of the moon.

"That video! Did you and Shane go out last night?"

"Yes. It was really scary. Coral, you heard the scream, right? And we couldn't see anyone, and—"

"Amy, you have to call the cops."

"Well, we already met one of Narrowdale's security guys, and he checked it out. He couldn't find anything."

"Did he call the cops?"

"He said he did." I flip another page. More pictures of the moon. I glance at Shane.

"That's a lot of moon in here," I say.

"What?" asks Coral. "What the hell are you talking about?"

"Yeah," says Shane. "I like the moon. I'm not sure why, but I really love capturing it. I take picture of it almost every week."

I shut the album and breathe deeply. I can hear Edgar's raspy voice in my mind. "Why does he like the moon so much?"

The smart thing to do is to ignore this. It's just another coincidence. I can go to LA on the weekend, rest a little, maybe have a serious talk with Mom and Dad and get some professional help. It's not a bad idea.

"Coral," I hear myself say. "Do you feel like meeting me near the shopping mall this afternoon?"

CHAPTER TWENTY-ONE

Coral's waiting for me at the bus station near the shopping mall, her bag on her shoulder.

"Hey," she says. "Do you feel like telling me what's going on?"

"In a minute. Shane is joining us as well."

"Joining us to do… what?"

"To talk to someone here."

"Amy… What's going on?"

"I had this… thing this morning. I don't know what to call it. It was like a hallucination. No, hang on. I'm not explaining myself well and I sound insane. It was like I was dreaming, but I was awake."

"Still sounding insane, Amy."

"Damn, this is hard. Me and Shane went to that street again this morning, the one where we heard the scream. And–"

"You really shouldn't be chasing strangers in the middle of the night. Especially not in Narrowdale."

"Yeah, fine, whatever. Anyway, I suddenly had this dream again, the one where I'm being chased. And I finally figured it out–it's the same street! I'm being chased on that exact street!"

"Okay… so what does it mean?"

"No idea!" I say unhappily. "But I hope to talk to someone who can shed some light on… Here's Shane!"

We wave at him and he jogs across the street and joins us.

"So, what are we doing here?" asks Shane.

"There's someone here that I want to talk to," I answer. "You'll see."

Shane glances at Coral, who shrugs. "I've got no idea," she says. "She dragged me over here with no explanation at all."

I ignore both of them, looking around me. The bus station is next to the parking lot, in front of the mall. The mall isn't big, and with a few dozen steps I reach the edge of the parking lot, and I spot him. He is looking through some large trash cans. He's muttering to himself grumpily, scrutinizing an old dirty newspaper. I begin walking towards him, Coral and Shane following me. My heart is beating rapidly as we get nearer, and I feel as if I'm split in two. Amy number one is trying to convince me to give this all up—it's all nonsense mixed up with stress. Amy number two is marching resolutely, intent on facing… whatever it is that needs to be faced. Amy number two wants to sleep at night, and she will not let Amy number one convince her otherwise.

Edgar turns to face us as we get closer. "I'm glad you could finally make it," he says. "Do you have some money?"

Amy number two is suddenly convinced that Amy number one is totally right. Really, Amy number two made a huge mistake, and she won't do it again. She swears she'll always listen to Amy number one, no matter what. Amy number one mentions that she hopes Amy number two is happy, because now it's too late to leave.

"We have no money." Shane waves his hand dismissively at Edgar.

"I have five dollars," I say shakily, pulling out my wallet.

Edgar smiles. "Nice girl," he says. "Not like your liar friend. It isn't nice to lie."

Shane stares at Edgar furiously. "Excuse me? Who do you think—"

"Shane," I interrupt. "This is Edgar. Edgar is a very nice man, who sometimes knows things."

Shane opens his mouth, then closes it, and his hand starts opening his camera's case.

"No filming please," says Edgar quickly. "I don't like it when parts of me are carried around in other people's cameras."

Shane drops his hand. I pull out two singles from my wallet and hand them over to Edgar.

"You said you had five dollars," he says sulkily.

"That's right. I have five dollars, but I want to buy myself something to eat later," I answer. "I am giving you two."

He nods, shoving the bills into his pocket. "True, I shouldn't be greedy. I can buy a nice roll for dinner with two dollars."

"Edgar," I say hesitantly. "Do you know about the whistling near my home?"

He waves his hand around, as if to swat a fly. "There's no whistling near your home."

"Oh," I say, feeling both relieved and disappointed. "Okay. I just thought–"

"There's whistling next to *her* home," he continues. "She thinks it's nothing–she'll be home soon, everything is all right. She really should have asked for a ride. It isn't good for a young lady to walk so late at night all alone. And the street lights aren't working, why is that?" He stares at the floor. "Maybe I should buy a small muffin instead of a roll. I like muffins."

"Who is it?" I plead. "Who thinks it will all be all right? What was the scream we heard? Who's whistling in the street at night?"

He shuts his eyes "I'm tired, and you really are asking a lot of questions. It isn't nice, flooding me with all those memories. Sad memories. She was so beautiful, and so clean." He starts walking away. "A muffin. I'll buy a muffin."

"Edgar, what's her name?" I call after him. "Where does she live?"

"A muffin is much sweeter than a roll. What was her name? Something… so sad." He turns to face us. "What's her name? Last time anyone called her by her name was nine years and seven months ago. Since then, no one called her. Hang on!" He takes a step towards us. "I know!"

I take a step back nervously. "Yes?"

"I think I'll buy a roll after all. Because sometimes a muffin is too sweet, and that's bad for the teeth, you know. It's important to keep your teeth in good shape." He walks away, muttering.

"Amy," Coral says in a wavering voice. "What was that?"

"That was Edgar," I answer hollowly. "And I am not sure what to do anymore."

"Who was he talking about? Who is that, who thinks she'll be home soon? Why are we talking to crazy people in the street?"

"Let's go sit somewhere. I'm tired."

"We can go to my place," offers Coral. "My mom will be happy to fix dinner for you guys as well."

The idea of meeting Coral's mother doesn't seem very alluring right now. I glance at Shane pleadingly.

"We can go to my place," he says. "My parents are at work. We could fix ourselves something to eat."

Coral hesitates. "My mom thinks I'm coming home. She already made dinner."

"Coral," I say. "If your mom sees me now, with dark circles and bloodshot eyes, wearing wrinkled clothes, she'll tell you not to play with me anymore. Listen, I need time away from parents."

"Fine, I'll call her," she says glumly. "I'll tell her we're having a study group. She'll be hurt that I didn't tell her before, but that's okay, I'll call her. It's just that… she doesn't like it when I miss dinner, but here, I'm calling her right now." She pulls out her phone and stares at it.

"Take your time," I tell her.

She sighs and dials. "Hey, Mom. Listen, I'm going to study with some friends. Yes, now. No, I know you've already made dinner, I just have to study. Really? Soup? Listen, Mom, just save a bowl for me. Yeah, in the fridge. I'll eat it when I get home. I know that it isn't the same as eating it fresh, but… no, it's fine, you can give my dessert to Dad. Yes, I'm sorry. Yes, next time I'll let you know. Yes, I remember I'm looking after Mia tonight. I'll be home by eight. Okay, half past seven. I'm sorry. Really? So long? I didn't know it's so hard making soup. Yes, next time. Sorry. Bye."Sshe hangs up.

"I hope you're happy," she tells me.

"Ecstatic," I answer. "Let's go to Shane's."

CHAPTER TWENTY-TWO

"So what do you want in your sandwich?" Shane calls from the kitchen.

"I want some cream cheese!" Coral calls back. "With some lettuce, if you have any!"

"We don't have lettuce," answers Shane, and after a moment adds, "or cream cheese."

I stare at Shane's computer screen. My head throbs, and I massage my temples, trying to think of a way to create some order in Edgar's inane drivel. What did he say exactly? She was beautiful, and clean–not very useful. Something about asking for a ride, about her being alone...

"Do you have ham?" Coral shouts, interrupting my thoughts.

"We're out."

"Uh... tuna?"

"Yep! Oh, hang on. I think it's a bit old. It's kinda dry in the corners. Do you mind?"

"Yes," sighs Coral. "I mind."

"Coral, could you please be quiet for a second? I'm trying to concentrate," I say.

"What are you doing?" she asks.

"Trying to figure out what it was that Edgar told us."

"I am making peanut-butter-and-jam sandwiches for us all," announces Shane.

"But–" Coral starts saying.

"That sounds great!" I yell, and add quietly. "Leave it. You won't eat dinner like your Mom makes. Not here."

"But peanut butter and jelly? For dinner?"

"Coral, please, just… Just let it go, okay?"

"Yeah, yeah, fine. So hang on, let me get this straight. Are you talking about that crazy homeless guy, who was talking about muffins and all sorts of nonsense? You want to figure out what he said?"

"He's not… well, I guess he is a crazy homeless guy. But I think he knows stuff. Stuff that other people don't know."

"Like what?"

"Like that thing he said. How did it go? Damn it! I've already forgotten everything he told us."

"She thinks it's nothing she'll be home soon, everything is all right. She really should have asked for a ride. It isn't good for a young lady to walk so late at night all alone," recites Coral.

I stare at her in surprise She shrugs. "What? It doesn't even come near to what I need to memorize for tests in English class."

"Okay," I say, full of admiration. "But it's still not enough. I know all that. More or less."

"Well, he was talking about muffins," she mentions.

"Thanks."

"And he said that the last time anyone called her by her name was nine years and seven months ago."

"That's right!" I type in "nine years and seven months" and press "search". The screen fills with useful links for articles about dog years, child development, something related to the constitution… I shut my eyes in despair. "This is not helping at all."

"What isn't helping?" Shane enters the room, holding a plate with three sandwiches.

"Amy is searching online for things related to what Edgar told us," explains Coral.

"Okay, so what did you search for?"

"He said that the last time anyone called her was nine years and seven months ago, so I searched for the term 'nine years and seven months,'" I say irritably. The sight of the sandwiches makes me understand that I have no appetite at all.

"Well, what did you expect?" asks Shane. "Who searches like that? Use the search with a date filter."

"What?"

"Look for something that happened nine years and seven months ago."

"How do I do that?"

"Move over."

I move over to the bed and Shane sits in front of the computer.

"What month was it nine years and seven months ago?" he asks.

"February," Coral answers with no hesitation.

"Okay." He selects the relevant date. "What should I look for?"

What should he look for? A ride? A clean girl? Let's start with something a bit... general. "Look for... Narrowdale," I tell him.

He types it in and presses "search." "There's nothing here." he says, after scanning the screen.

"What's that?" Coral points at the screen.

"That's an article about some clogging in Narrowdale's sewer," he answers.

"It might be related," she says.

I raise an eyebrow. "I don't think so," I say.

"Come on, click it," she insists.

"Okay, okay." He clicks the link. "It says that the clogging was fixed."

"Excellent," I mutter.

"Add the word 'night' to the search," says Coral.

"Why?" He looks at her skeptically.

"What do you mean, why?" She sounds annoyed. "Edgar said it was night, In Amy's dreams it's always night... will you just do it?"

I don't recall seeing Coral so determined. Where did it come from? Shane turns back to the computer and does what he's told. The screen fills with links again, and suddenly I tense up.

"What's that?" I ask.

"It's nothing," he answers. "just some woman complaining that her neighbor is very noisy at night..."

"Not that! Three links down!"

"Oh yeah, hang on." She clicks the link. "Here we go. It says that a woman disappeared in the middle of the night in Narrowdale, and that the police are looking for her. The article is dated... February, nine years ago."

"Nine years and seven months ago," says Coral.

My heart is pounding. "What's her name?" I ask.

He reads silently for a moment. "Kimberly," he finally answers. "Kimberly White."

"Kimberly White," I repeat, the sound of high heels tapping on the sidewalk echoing in my ears. "We know what happened to her."

"It doesn't say here what happened to her," says Shane, sounding far away.

"But we know what happened to her," I say, shivering. It's so cold. "She was walking alone, at night, in the dark. She should have asked for a ride. It's scary, being alone in the street at night..."

I stop, breathing deeply. I can see my breath in the cold night's air. "Kimberly White wore high-heel shoes which tapped on the sidewalk as she walked. She wore a coat. It was the middle of the winter, and it was very cold. Kimberly senses that someone is following her and she starts walking faster." Who am I talking to? I can no longer remember. "The street lights don't work. Darkness surrounds me, and I feel as if someone is following me. I don't want to hurry, but I can feel my legs moving faster, I'm scared..."

"Amy..." I can hear a voice from far away, a familiar voice. Who is trying to talk to me?

There is someone behind me, and he starts to whistle. His whistle echoes around me, shrill, creepy. I'll be home soon. Mustn't run, mustn't run. I think he is getting closer; his whistle sounds much louder, I can't take it anymore, I start running, he stops whistling, but I can hear his footsteps behind me, I think he's catching up. I don't know what to do! My ankle twists, I trip, someone grabs my hair and whispers...

"Don't cry sweetheart...," I say in a gravelly voice. "We are together at last."

My eyes open. Shane and Coral are staring at me, terrified. What happened? Where did I go? Was it me who spoke just now? Or was it Kimberly White's pursuer from that night? What is happening to me? I start sobbing, and I feel Coral's arms wrap around me in a tight hug.

CHAPTER TWENTY-THREE

By the time I get back home, the sun is setting. Fortunately, Mom and Dad haven't returned yet, and I don't have to explain why I was wandering outside when I claim to be sick. I fry myself a nice omelet. Mom arrives home just after I start, so I fry one for her as well, because I am such a wonderful daughter.

"Are you feeling better?" Mom asks.

"Not really. I still feel shitty."

She puts her hand on my forehead. "You have no fever," she rules. Mom's just like that. If you have no fever, it's not a real sickness. "If you don't have any fever tomorrow, I want you to go to school."

"Fine." I burn the omelet a little. Mom is chopping a small salad as I struggle with the frying pan.

"So what did you do today?" she asks, getting us a couple of forks and knives.

"I don't know. I slept. Watched TV."

"Did someone update you on whatever you missed in school?"

"Sure, Mom, all the students from my class came over together. There weren't enough chairs for them all to sit."

Mom looks at me sympathetically. "Isn't that girl… what's her name again?"

"Coral."

"Isn't she in some of your classes?"

"Yeah." But we were busy talking to crazy homeless people and being possessed by ghosts. "Yeah, I'll talk to her."

"Good. You'll be happy to hear that the air conditioner is fixed."

"Happy? Understatement of the year, Mom! Really?" I get up and run to the control unit. I press the button excitedly. For a moment I think it isn't working. Then I realize that it is, and it's just so very quiet.

"Mom," I whisper. "Can you hear that?"

"Hear what, sweetie?"

"Exactly." I grin.

"I'm glad that you approve. Come back here and finish your dinner."

We begin to eat. Dad joins us after ten minutes, complaining about traffic. He asks if he can have an omelet as well. Feeling like the world is a better place, my parents are wonderful people, and everyone should really be nicer to each other, I make him one, and we all sit together to eat in our nice, pleasantly cool home.

Once I'm done I go to my room and browse the net. I look for the article about Kimberly White and locate it quickly. It is pretty concise. Kimberly's mom is asking people to call her if anyone saw her daughter, or knows something about her disappearance. Below the article's text there is a small picture of Kimberly, smiling. I examine the photo, troubled. There is something... familiar in her face. It feels as if I've seen her before. A phone number is noted in the article. I dial the number anxiously, but it seems to be disconnected.

I begin to nod off, but I really don't want to fall asleep. I can't handle any more nightmares. I play some idiotic games on the net to stay awake. Apparently, I manage to find a cow and it is added to my farm. Sounds like cattle theft to me, but who am I to judge? At around eleven I creep down to the kitchen. Mom and Dad are already asleep. I pour myself some hot water and get the coffee jar from the cupboard.

It's not that I'm not allowed to drink coffee, but that's just because the subject never came up. I'm pretty sure Mom would have plenty to say if she saw me drinking coffee in the middle of the night, so I do my best to do it as quietly as possible. I make it like Mom drinks it, with a really large spoonful of coffee and half a cup of hot water. I sip carefully.

Yuck.

I decide that adding sugar might be a good idea. I add two spoonfuls, and after a moment add two more, just in case. I taste it again. Sickening, but drinkable. I take the mug back to my room. I drink the entire thing as I watch YouTube clips.

My phone rings. It's Nicole.

"Hey, Nicole, why are you calling so late at night?"

"What time should I be calling? When I call during the day you're always busy."

"Yeah, you're right," I sigh. "Sorry, I'm just having a rough couple of days."

"Do you want to talk about it?"

"I… I'd rather not talk about it in the middle of the night. It creeps me out enough as it is." I take another mouthful of the horrid brew.

"What're you drinking?"

"Coffee."

A short pause. "Coffee?" she asks. "Since when do you drink coffee?"

"Since now. Coffee is disgusting."

"It is. And you're not supposed to drink it in the middle of the night. You won't be able to fall asleep!"

"That's the idea. So, tell me what happened with Jack."

"He called." She sounds excited. "He said we haven't spoken in ages, and he wants to see me."

"Really?" I smile. "And what did you say?"

"What do you think I said? Do you remember how he looks? I said sure."

"Even if I didn't remember how he looks, I've heard you describe him at least seven times."

"And he's fifteen, and he's about to get his motorcycle driver's license. He said he has enough money to buy a used motorcycle once he gets his license. Isn't it awesome?"

"Sure, but Nicky, don't throw yourself at him just because he looks great and will have a motorcycle someday."

"Honey, I'm throwing myself at him because he's the most amazing guy in the world, and he wants to see me. We have a date for Saturday night."

"Saturday night... Hang on, I'm visiting you on the weekend!"

"You'll join us, honey. It'll be awesome."

"Because nothing says awesome more than being a third wheel. Never mind, I'll go to one of the Jennifers during your date. What did your mom say?"

"Do you really think I asked her? What about you? Who is that Shane guy?"

"Shane? Just someone from school that I'm friends with."

"Just friends? Honey, what's going on with you? I'm sure there are great guys in Narrowdale."

"There are," I agree. "I found one."

"Really? From school?"

"No. He graduated."

"Amy..."

"He's a security guy here. He's handsome and cute, and manly–"

"Amy! How old is he?"

"I don't know... nineteen?"

"And you're dating him?"

"Not exactly..."

"Amy, you can't fall in love with someone who's nineteen!"

"Why not?"

"Because it will end in tears," she sighs. "Find someone in school. Someone cute, and funny, the type you like..."

"Sounds good. Can you give me Jack's phone number?"

"You're a real riot, honey, I simply can't stop laughing."

"How are Scott and Williams?"

"They're fine, honey. You know what Jennifer S. told me?"

The conversation flows on, and reminds me how much I love talking to Nicole. Funny, lighthearted Nicole, who loves me so much. Always happy and optimistic, always knows how to cheer me up. We finish talking once she falls asleep in the middle of a sentence.

The coffee is working, no doubt about it. I'm starting to feel more alert and full of energy. I browse a little more, looking for information about Kimberly, finding nothing of interest. I read additional articles from nine years ago. The sewage clog was indeed fixed, to the residents' immense relief. The local football team lost to Florence's team. The mayor announced the construction of a huge shopping mall, which would change the face of Narrowdale. Thinking about the shopping mall, I wonder if the mayor is disappointed by the result.

I decide to look for Kimberly's mom. Her first name is Patricia, and I'm guessing her surname is White. I find some unrelated articles about different Patricia Whites. One Patricia White has several posts in a forum for pregnant women. A second Patricia just saw that girl who plays Rachel in *Glee* at a restaurant. A woman named Patricia Collins says that white clothes can be washed at a high temperature with vinegar to remove certain stains.

Something is trickling down my cheek. Something wet and warm. It's blood. I remember, I hit my head. I am bleeding. I feel it reaching my chin, dripping to the floor. I can't talk–something is blocking my mouth. I can't move–my hands are bound behind my back, and my feet are bound as well.

How long have I been here? Hours? A day, maybe two? How many times did he come in, whistling his eerie tune, whispering creepy sentences?

I'm cold. I'm still wearing my coat, but I'm cold. I don't feel so good. I'm weak, my head is spinning. I must get out of here before he returns, I must. I struggle against the ropes binding my hands. It hurts, they scratch my hands, but I have to go on, I have to get out of here, how can I…

The rope loosens a little. I can do this.

I tug harder. My left hand is almost free. It burns terribly. I can feel all my skin tearing off. I have to free it… footsteps, and that whistling once more. The door opens, and the light beyond it blinds me. I can barely see his silhouette in the doorway…

I wake up from the repeated beeping from my laptop. I fell asleep on the keyboard. Apparently my last search query was:
rtttttttttttttttttttttttttttttttttttttttttttttttttttttttttttttttttttttttttttttttttttttttttttttttttttttttttttt.

It's two fifty-two a.m. I sit in the darkness, staring at the screen, recalling the feeling of rough ropes binding my hands, the eerie sound of blood dripping on the floor. Four more hours until sunrise.
http://amy.strangerealm.com/awake.html

CHAPTER TWENTY-FOUR

I get off the bus completely exhausted and start walking in a generally straight line towards school. Clearly my body can't take much more of this. I nearly reach the school gate when Coral grabs me and drags me aside.

"You look awful," she informs me.

"Gee, thanks."

"I found Kimberly White's mother."

This manages to enliven me a little. "Patricia White? Really?"

"Yes. Come on." She leads me down the street.

"School's the other way," I point out.

"We're not going to school," she answers. "You're not in any condition to be at school. You'll just fall asleep and wake up screaming in class again."

"But... they might teach something important."

"They might," she agrees.

"The teacher might take attendance."

"That's certainly a possibility."

"Who are you, and what did you do with Coral?"

"Call Shane. Ask him to meet us in the coffee shop down the street, if he can."

I obediently call Shane. He promises that he'll get there as soon as possible. I am dragging my friends down the path to delinquency.

Coral walks resolutely to the local coffee shop, a place called "Barbar Koffee," and pushes me inside. I look around me. The place looks really strange. It's as if someone woke up one day thinking, "I know I meant to go to the beach today… but perhaps I should open a coffee shop instead." The chairs are mismatched, some plastic, some wooden and one that looks like an office chair with small squeaky wheels. There are plants everywhere, but they are all growing inside used coffee and jam jars; there is not one actual flower pot in sight. The decoration is a mix between photos of places around the world and some weird abstract paintings which hang crookedly, as if someone couldn't bother putting them straight. If I took Nicole here, she would refuse to cross the place's threshold. We sit down at a table which looks as if it was once a writing desk.

"This place is…" I look for the right word. "Quaint?"

Coral shrugs. "It's been here since forever."

"Really? Okay. I have no money with me," I say.

"No problem, I'll pay,"

"I'll repay you tomorrow."

"I'm buying. You don't need to pay me back."

"So… Are you incredibly rich or something?"

The waitress approaches us.

"I would like a blueberry muffin and hot chocolate, please," Coral says.

"Just coffee for me," I say.

"What kind of coffee?"

I stare at her. "Are there different kinds?"

"Black coffee, cappuccino, espresso…," she starts listing.

"Um… Cappuccino, please."

Coral raises an eyebrow as the waitress wanders off. "Do you drink coffee?"

"Oh, absolutely. Since yesterday. Want to know a secret? Coffee is disgusting."

"So you're a masochist. I couldn't tell. Okay. So, to make a long story short, I called the newspaper where we saw the article…"

"It wasn't a newspaper, it was online," I say, trying to annoy her.

"Right, on the website of the local newspaper. So I called…."

"How does one call a newspaper? Sounds like a silly thing to do."

"I called the editorial department of the newspaper. Don't be a pain. I asked to talk to Gwen Mitchell–"

"Who's Gwen Mitchell?"

"The reporter who wrote the article."

"How do you know?"

Shane enters the coffee shop and approaches us. Coral moves her chair a bit, and he picks up a chair from a different table and places it next to hers.

"What's up?" he says.

"Coral talked to Gwen Mitchell," I reply.

"Who's Gwen Mitchell?"

"The reporter who wrote the article we read yesterday," she explains once more.

"How do you know?"

"Her name was at the top of the article. Anyway, to make a long story short, she still works there, luckily for us. She is now the senior editor or something. So I told her I'm working on a school project about Narrowdale's history, and asked if she knows what happened with Kimberly White's case."

"And what did she say?" asks Shane, fascinated.

"Well, she dug up some material in her archives–"

"I'm surprised she didn't hang up in your face," I interrupt her.

"I can be incredibly charming and cute when I want to."

"Hard to believe."

The waitress approaches us and serves Coral a muffin and hot chocolate. She then puts in front of me a cup of strangely white coffee. I add four packets of sugar to the cup, ignoring the unbelieving stares around me.

"I like it sweet," I explain to the waitress.

"I can see that." She turns to address Shane. "Would you like anything?"

"A glass of water, thanks."

"Mineral water?"

"No. I'd like tap water please."

The waitress leaves.

"To make a long story short–" Coral says once more.

"This long story is not short at all," I complain. "Why do you keep saying that?"

"Gwen Mitchell said that they never found Kimberly. She suggested I talk to Kimberly's mom."

"But the number in the article is disconnected," I say. "We have no way to reach her." I take a sip from my cappuccino. Ick.

"We have one now." She pulls a note from her pocket and hands it to me. Shane leans over the table to see what it is.

"Is that her address?" I squint. "Washington Street? Where's that?"

"I checked the map–" Coral begins.

"It's the street just across from the one where we heard the scream," Shane interrupts her.

"Right." Coral looks irritated. "Well, anyway, I printed a map. You probably don't need it as you seem to know where it is, but just in case, I have it here. In my backpack."

"Do you think we should talk to her?" I ask.

"Don't you?" She seems surprised.

"Is it such a good idea?" I ask. "It was ten years ago. Why should we bring back bad memories? This poor woman probably lost her daughter… Anyway, what are we going to tell her?"

"We can start by asking her if her daughter was ever found," Shane says quietly. "If she was, we're just digging up a non-story. Didn't you say you want this thing over?"

"I did."

"Then let's get it over with."

"Yeah, okay."

The waitress puts a glass of tap water in front of Shane.

"Check, please," says Coral.

CHAPTER TWENTY-FIVE

Washington Street is somewhere between my home and the coffee house, and Patricia's house is located on its far end. We manage to find it without any problem. I suspect that Coral was here already and made sure she knew exactly where it was. Of course, finding the house is the easy part.

"Okay, so... here's the house," I say weakly. Shane nods, handling his camera nervously. He takes a quick photo of the front yard.

"Yup," says Coral and approaches the front door, about to knock.

"Hang on!" I say, panicking. What are we even doing here? What will we tell her? That I'm dreaming about her daughter every night? That a homeless person near the mall hinted to us about her? It was a mistake coming here... But Coral is already knocking on the door. We wait quietly for a few seconds. "Maybe she moved," I suggest.

"Could be," nods Coral.

"Or she's not at home," I say.

"It's possible, but knock again," says Shane.

Coral knocks once more, and a moment later we can hear footsteps approaching from within. The door opens, and there she is. Patricia White. I immediately know it's her, though I've never seen her before. There's something in her eyes. Something familiar... and sad.

"Hello, are you Mrs. Patricia White?" Coral asks.

"Yes," Patricia answers, her tone curious. "Who are you?"

"My name is Coral, and these are my friends, Amy and Shane. Can you spare a few minutes to talk to us?"

"What's this about?"

"We're high school students here in Narrowdale," says Coral. "and we are working on a school project. The topic is police effectiveness in the area." Me and Shane exchange disbelieving looks. How did she come up with this?

"And how can I help you?" asks Patricia.

"We wanted to know if we can ask you a few questions about your daughter, Kimberly."

Silence. I struggle with an overwhelming need to run away, leave this entire thing behind me. Why did we have to come to this house, awaken painful memories? What did I think this would accomplish?

"Follow me," says Patricia, her voice a bit chilly. "We can sit in the porch."

We follow her through a small and tidy yard around to the back of the house. There's a wooden porch there, with a table and several chairs. Patricia sits on one of them, and we sit in front of her, the table standing between us. After a moment she stands up.

"It's hot outside. Would you like some water?" she asks.

"Yes, please." Coral smiles. Patricia turns around and walks inside.

"Shane!" Coral says, eyeing him angrily. "Can you please stop taking pictures?"

"Why?"

"Because it isn't polite!"

He shrugs. "We might want to look at those pictures later. You can tell her it's part of our school project."

"Yeah, Coral, what the hell was that gibberish?" I hiss at her.

"Do you have a better story?" she asks. "Do you want to talk to her about your dreams?"

"No, but—"

Patricia walks out of the house, carrying a tray with four glasses of water. She places it on the table and sits. Coral leans forward, takes a glass of water and drinks from it. She seems completely comfortable, as if she interviews mothers with long lost daughters for a living.

"Mrs. White—" Coral starts to say.

"Patricia," Patricia says. "You can call me Patricia."

"Patricia, would you mind if we take some photos for our project?"

"No, I don't mind."

She looks at us, and I know that she doesn't want us to take any photos, doesn't want to tal to us at all. But Coral and Shane seem satisfied, and Shane takes picture of me, Coral and Patricia.

"Patricia, I'm sorry, bu can you please tell us what happened to your daughter?"

"Kimberly disappeared over nine years ago," answers Patricia, her voice dry and hollow, as if she's reciting a memorized text. "She went to meet some friends. Her friends said she left just past midnight, but she never came back home."

"Where were they?" I ask, unable to stop myself.

"At her friend's home," answers Patricia. "Not far from here."

"Where exactly?" I ask.

"On Oak Street."

"And what did you do when you realized she was missing?" Coral asks.

"The next morning, when I saw she hadn't returned, I called all of her friends. Then I called the police."

"And how did the police react?" Coral asks.

"Two officers came here and asked me some questions. There was a search. They sometimes updated me regarding their progress."

"And… Did they find anything?" I ask, my throat dry.

Patricia looks at me, and I suddenly get the feeling that she knows. Knows everything. About the dreams, about Edgar, about the whistle. I swallow nervously.

"No," Patricia says, and for the first time since we got here, her dry voice cracks a little. "Kimberly simply disappeared."

We all stay silent. Coral looks as if she's struggling to find something to say. Patricia picks up one of the glasses on the tray, stares at it, brings it closer to her mouth, then changes her mind and puts it back on the tray.

"I'm sorry to ask…," I stutter. "Did Kimberly have any… peculiar friends? Perhaps some guy who seemed a bit weird?"

"Not at all. All her friends were very nice."

"In the days before the… disappearance, did you hear any whistling or… anything out of the ordinary?" I continue, desperate to find a clue that will help me understand what had happened that day.

"No…," she frowns. "But I don't understand what that's got to do with your school project."

"On that night, maybe you heard–"

"Amy!" Coral interrupts me. "This really has nothing to do with our project." She looks at me meaningfully, but I can't stop myself. "But Coral, maybe she heard–"

Coral turns back to Patricia, talking loudly over me "Mrs. White, when did you last talk to the police?"

"About a year and a half after she disappeared. A cop called to tell me they'd update me if they encountered any new leads. I haven't heard from them since."

"I see. And during the time they handled your daughter's case, were there any–"

"I'm sorry, I have nothing else to say." Patricia interrupts her and stands up. I can see the pain flooding her eyes, as I knew it would. We should never have come here. "I would rather wrap this up. I… I have to go."

We all stand up, embarrassed.

"Mrs. White, thanks for everything," Coral says. Patricia nods and escorts us out to the street. Saying nothing, she turns back to the house, walks in, and shuts the door behind her.

CHAPTER TWENTY-SIX

It's dark. My head is pounding. Someone hit it, I suddenly remember. I'm shivering. It's so cold here, in this dark room. How long have I been here? A day? Two? How many times did he walk in, whisper in my ear? How many times have I tried to talk to him, beg for my life, muffled by the rag stuck in my mouth?

My hands are throbbing. Why is that? Oh right, I am trying to get loose and the rope is peeling my skin. Are the knots slightly looser, or is it just my imagination? I won't be able to stay here much longer. I'm hungry, freezing, and afraid of what will happen the next time he walks in. I have to try once more.

I start struggling again. I can feel the rope tearing my hand, but I force myself to ignore the pain, carry on... one hand is loose!

I remove the rag from my mouth. I can move my jaw freely. I open and close my mouth a few times, loosening it up. My trembling hands begin to untie the rope binding my legs. It's much harder than I thought it would be. My hands are bleeding and cold; they feel numb and move slowly. The knot is tight... I finally manage to untie it.

My heart is beating fast. I might manage to escape, and with this slight hope comes fear. What if he walks in right now? What if he catches me? Perhaps I should wait, holding something heavy behind the door, attack him as he walks in? No. I am weak with hunger and exhaustion, and he is bigger and stronger than me. I must escape.

I move slowly, feeling around with my hands, walking alongside the room's walls. My hand touches something cold and smooth–glass. This is a window! But why is there no light coming through? Could it be so dark outside? It doesn't matter. My hand slides across the window carefully, finding the handle, turning it slowly. It's stuck, and I twist it harder. The window opens with a horrible screeching sound. He probably heard it, I must hurry! Behind the window there's some sort of thick cloth, I push at it and it tears. Sunlight comes through, blinding me.

Footsteps down the hall behind me. He's coming! I leap through the window, but my legs are tired and hurt, and I stumble. The top half of my body is outside, in the sunlight, but the legs are still inside. The light is so bright and it's hard to see but it looks like a small backyard. I struggle to get out, kicking with my legs, trying to push my body out. Nearly there... My eyes are getting used to the light, and I start to notice small details. A small vegetable garden, a scarecrow standing in the middle, flowers all around... I hear the door behind me open. He is shouting, but I can't understand what he's saying.

A hand grabs my leg. I scream, kick with my second leg, and hear him cry in pain. I try to wriggle outside, but he won't let go. He pulls me back. My hands search for something to grab at, anything at all, but find nothing. Somewhere in the distance, a dog is barking.

He pulls me in, and I fall on the floor. From the corner of my eye I can still see the open window, the twinkling sunlight, but he is standing above me, a huge angry shadow, screaming senseless sentences about my ingratitude, my traitorous actions. He swings something large in his hand, and it hurtles towards my face...

My eyes open wide. I am lying in my bed, full of frustration and despair. Almost! I've almost managed to escape! I breathe deeply, try to relax, remind myself that it's just a dream. I get up, approach the window. The neighbor's dog is standing outside, barking. When I open my window she whines strangely.

"Quiet!" I tell her. Why doesn't the neighbor take her in?

Alex's front door opens and he steps out.

"Moka!" he says. "Quiet! Come inside!" He turns his head up and our eyes meet. I step away from the window quickly. I'm not sure what I saw in his gaze, but I don't like it.

I call Coral. I wait anxiously with the phone at my ear and have nearly given up when I suddenly hear her drowsy voice.

"Amy? What time is it?"

"I don't know," I say. "It's the middle of the night."

"Okay," she yawns. "I was sleeping. Is it important?"

"I just wanted to talk to you," I answer. "I had a bad dream."

"Again?"

"It was different from the other nightmares. I nearly… It was different."

"Then let's talk about it tomorrow at school," she says. "I want to go back to sleep."

"Maybe we can skip school tomorrow…," I begin hopefully.

"No," she interrupts. "Not again. I don't like lying to my Mom, and I don't like missing class, and I keep thinking that I'm going to be caught. I'm going to school."

"Fine." I sigh. "We'll meet tomorrow."

"Okay. Amy, will you be able to fall asleep?"

"I don't think I am going to try. I've slept enough for one night."

"Sleep is important," she reminds me.

"Good night, Coral."

"Good night."

I contemplate calling Shane, but Coral's tired reaction makes me think that perhaps talking to him in the morning might be more productive. The rest of the night is spent in front of my laptop. What would I do without Internet?

CHAPTER TWENTY-SEVEN

"Good morning," Mom says as I drag myself into the kitchen. "How are you feeling this morning?"

"Better," I mumble, filling the kettle with water.

"Really?" she says, scrutinizing me. "You don't look so good."

"I didn't sleep well."

"Didn't you sleep with the air conditioning on?"

"Yeah." I find a mug, put one spoonful of instant coffee and three spoonfuls of sugar.

"I don't want you to drink coffee, Amy. It isn't healthy for a girl your age."

"Just this morning okay? I don't want to fall asleep during school. After today, I won't drink any more. I promise."

She looks as if she's about to argue, but finally she sighs. "Fine," she says. "Just this morning."

"Nicole invited me to stay with her this weekend," I say. "Can I go there tomorrow?"

"Sure," Mom nods. "It will be good for you to see your friends again. I'll drive you."

"Thanks."

I sip some coffee. I'm definitely getting used to it. I force myself to eat some cereal for breakfast. After finishing half a bowl, I pour the rest down the sink and start walking up to my room. The dripping noise makes me stop.

Dripping. I recall the blood pooling on the dirty floor of the dark room. A drop of blood trickling down my cheek, dripping into the same pool. I freeze and open my ears. The dripping sound continues, behind the storage room door. I can feel the fear crawling up my back. I stumble to the door and open it.

The same storage room, full with my parents' stuff. No blood. The floor is a bit dusty, and it doesn't look like the grimy floor from my dream at all. The dripping sound stops. I must be going insane.

I close the door, walk up to the bathroom, brush my teeth and leave.

"Good morning," says Alex the neighbor as I walk out the door.

"Good morning," I reply warily.

"Did Moka wake you up?"

"Yes, she keeps barking at night."

"There are things in the darkness that Moka doesn't like," he says, "so she barks."

"Yes. And it wakes me up."

"It is sometimes a good thing to wake up," he looks at me intently. "And sometimes it is good to leave old memories alone."

I feel as if I'm drenched in cold water. "I have to go," I say. "I'm late for the school bus."

I walk quickly towards the bus stop. What did he mean? I recall the shadow from my dreams. A towering figure, whispering creepy sentences, shouting angrily... could he be...?

I notice the bus at the stop. I have to run to catch up with it. I reach it breathing hard, and the driver glowers at me as he closes the door after me. I turn to sit down. Jasmine, sitting in her seat in the front, looks at me in contempt.

"There she goes," she says. "The local security guy's damsel in distress."

I stare at her and suddenly realize something remarkable. Underneath the sarcasm, hatred and nastiness in her voice there's a hint of... jealousy? For a moment I forget about Alex, forget about Kimberly, forget about my dreams. What would Nicole do?

"Don't worry," I hear myself say. "I'm sure that once your breasts start to grow, once you find a way to get rid of your bad breath, and once you get that nice mustache under control, you'll find someone to take some interest in you too."

She becomes pale, and her eyes narrow. For the first time in weeks I feel victorious. I pass her by as she is trying to work out a snappy comeback and sit down in the rear of the bus.

I manage to sleep the entire ride to school without dreaming, which is quite an accomplishment, and I'm very pleased with myself as I get off the bus.

My first class today is Spanish. I am already fostering a deep hatred for the Spanish teacher. This is not due to any special reason beyond one fact–she insists on teaching us Spanish. As far as I am concerned, this is completely inexcusable. Today she is reading us a paragraph about "*el profesor*". Apparently he is "*muy importante.*" In less than three minutes she loses me completely, and "*el profesor*" can go to "*el*" as far as I'm concerned.

The bell announces the end of the class. Second class–Math. I walk to the classroom and sit down next to Coral.

"Hey," I say. "Sorry for waking you up."

"No problem." She smiles. "I think that I was nodding off during most of our conversation. I fell asleep immediately afterward."

"Good," I say, irritated. I wouldn't wish the last few nights upon my friends, but it would be nice if they'd avoid telling me how wonderfully they slept.

"So what did you dream?" she asks.

"I dreamt I nearly managed to escape," I say. Mrs. Mermenstein, our infamous teacher, walks in and tells us all to open our notebooks.

"I was tied up in a dark room," I whisper to Coral. "But I managed to loosen the ropes that bound me."

"Great," she whispers back. "Let's talk about it later."

"There was a window in the room," I continue, "and when I opened it–"

"Amy!" Mrs. Mermenstein shouts. "Be quiet and open your notebook!"

I'm not sure I brought any notebook.

"Anyway," I carry on with a hushed tone, ignoring the frightened glances Coral is sending towards the teacher. "I managed to open the window, and I was nearly outside–"

"Amy and Coral!" Mrs. Mermenstein yells. "I won't ask you to be quiet again!"

I fall silent. Coral's face becomes crimson. Mrs. Mermenstein turns to the whiteboard and begins to write something on it.

"He grabbed me!" I whisper. "He grabbed my leg, and–"

"Amy! Get out, immediately!" Mrs. Mermenstein screams. Coral looks as if she is about to cry. I get out, leaving my bag behind me. A minute later I regret leaving it, as my phone is inside, but I can't walk inside to get it. I pace around the empty corridors, thinking about the neighbor, about my nightmare, about Kimberly White... Suddenly it hits me. I now know why her picture looked so familiar. I run to the corridor where I ended up in the first day, the one with all the pictures. She looks at me with big, sad eyes. The girl that I thought was just some random, outstanding student. Kimberly White.

I examine the photo closely. As I'd noticed before, it's a bit blurry. They've probably taken an old photograph of her and enlarged it. And that figure in the background... Strange. I remember it much further back. It's almost as if it... came closer. No. It's coming closer. Right now. The figure becomes larger and larger, looming behind Kimberly, his face dark, his hands raised menacingly. Kimberly keeps looking forward with the same sad eyes. She can't hear him, can't see him, he's going to get her soon! He's right behind her, his shadow darkening the entire photograph...

Someone is sobbing. It's me. I turn and stumble away, shutting my eyes. I run to the bathroom and barge in, grasping one of the sinks. Something physical, something real. I really did see it. I'm not going crazy; it really happened. I wash my face, trying to calm my shivering hands.

Maybe it happened. Maybe not. Maybe it was just a shadow, something in the light of the corridor. Photographs do not come to life.

I can hear the bell ringing. I run back to math class and catch Coral just as she's leaving.

"Something happened just now!" I tell Coral, walking up to her. "I found a photograph of Kimberly in one of the hallways and–"

"What's wrong with you?" Coral asks me, her voice quivering. "Why did you have to talk about it during the class? Couldn't your dream wait for one hour? You know how important it is for me to concentrate in class..."

I stare at her in confusion. "But my dream is important. And I just saw–"

"It's just a dream! It can wait until the end of the class!"

"It's not just a dream!" I yell. People are looking at us. "It happened! It really happened! Kimberly White was kidnapped nine and a half years ago! She found herself tied up in a dark room and–"

"Amy, you don't even know that. It's just a guess..."

"It's not a guess," I hiss in anger. "It really happened. And you know what I think? I think you don't really care about concentrating in class. What you really care about is not having the teacher shouting at you. You're just a coward!" I stop walking. Coral hastens her steps and enters her next class.

The bell rings. I can't face another class, and I consider skipping school completely, when I notice Shane. He seems to be hurrying to class, already late.

"Shane!" I call, and join him.

"Hey, can we talk later? I'm really late–" he starts.

"I need you to see something," I interrupt him.

"Can't it wait?"

"No."

"Um... Yeah, sure. Okay."

I drag him to the corridor with Kimberly's photograph.

"Hey, that's a photograph of Kimberly White," he says.

I don't answer, simply stare at it in shock. Kimberly's looking at the camera, just as before, but her eyes are not sad at all. She is smiling. And behind her... there's no one. No shadow, no figure.

"She must have gone to school here, and they put up a photograph of her."

"Yeah," I say dully. "After she disappeared."

Shane takes a few steps back and snaps a picture of the photograph with his camera.

"Come on," he says. "I guess I'm already too late. Let's find somewhere to sit down."

"I had another dream," I say as we walk away from the photograph.

"Anything new?"

"Yes." I hesitate. "I nearly managed to escape. That means that Kimberly nearly managed to escape. I think."

"Really?" he says, and then points at an empty classroom. "There. Let's go in there."

We walk inside and pull up two chairs.

"Shane, do you think my dreams are just dreams?" I ask, worried.

He looks surprised. "I don't know," he answers. "It would be quite a coincidence, wouldn't it? You dreaming the same dream repeatedly, and Kimberly…"

"Yeah, but…. We don't really know it's related," I say. "So Kimberly went missing a few years ago. And I am having some weird dreams. But we don't really know it's connected–"

"And what about the whistles?" he interrupts me. "And that weird thing where you started talking as if you were possessed when you were in my room?"

"The whistling could be just… whistling. And I might be one card short of a full deck."

"One card short…?"

"You know… crazy. Nuts."

"Amy, what's wrong?" he asks.

"I don't know. Before, in the corridor, I saw… never mind. And I went ballistic at Coral. I think I made her cry. I'm so obsessed with this whole thing, I can't see straight. What if I'm imagining it all? Maybe it's just… I don't know. Stress."

"I think you're dreaming something that really happened," he interrupts me.

I exhale in relief. "Good. But what if you're wrong?"

He shrugs. "I don't think I'm wrong."

I lean back and shut my eyes.

"Why me?" I ask.

"What do you mean?"

"Why is it me who's dreaming about Kimberly? Why do I experience again and again what happened to her that night? What is the connection between me and her?"

"I don't know," says Shane. "You do kind of look like her."

"What?" I look at him in surprise.

"At least it seems that way from the picture in the article."

"Bullshit," I say nervously. "We're completely different. Our hair color isn't the same, our haircut is completely different, she's older than me…"

"I don't know, there's still something there. Maybe it's the eyes."

"That's just nonsense. I know exactly how I look. There's no similarity. You're just delusional."

"But–"

"Never mind that," I shake my head. "Let's talk about the night she disappeared. I want to keep digging at this."

"Okay," says Shane.

"You know what we need?" I say. "We need to go and talk with Kimberly's friends. The ones she was visiting that night. What did Patricia say their names were?"

"We didn't ask her."

I raise my eyebrows. "We didn't ask?"

"I'm pretty sure we didn't."

"How could we forget?"

"Amy, we aren't homicide detectives. This whole thing is pretty intense…"

"I have her phone number," I recall. "I asked for it before we left. I can simply call her and ask."

"There, you see?" he smiles. "No problem."

I take out my phone, find Patricia White in my contact list and dial. After a few seconds a woman answers.

"Hello," I say. "Patricia?"

"No," the woman says. "Wrong number."

"Sorry," I apologize and hang up.

"Damn," I mutter. "I think I wrote down the wrong number. I'll try again." I call once more.

"Hello," the same woman answers.

"Hi," I say. "Sorry, it's me again. I'm looking for Patricia. Patricia White. I guess I have the wrong number…"

"Patricia White?" says the woman. "No, you have the correct phone number. This was her house."

"Was?" I ask in confusion.

"Patricia White died seven years ago," the woman says.

"But… That can't be."

"I'm telling you, Patricia White is deceased," says the woman. "I bought this house from her family after she passed away."

"But I just met her!"

"Then you probably met a different Patricia, and this is the wrong number," the woman says impatiently.

"The Patricia White I'm talking about lives in Washington Street, Narrowdale," I say.

"Yes, that's my address." The woman sounds suspicious. "I'm sorry, what's your name again? Who gave you my address?"

"I got it from… but… What did she die of?"

"She lost her daughter, and her health declined rapidly afterwards," she answers. "Who am I talking to?"

I hang up.

"Shane," I whisper. "Patricia White is dead."

"Oh my god!" he says, horrified. "How did it happen?"

"She died seven years ago. Health problems."

Shane looks completely confused. "Then who did we talk to yesterday?"

"I have no idea."

CHAPTER TWENTY-EIGHT

The final class today is English. When I enter the classroom I notice that Coral has moved her bag to a vacant seat in the back of the room. I think of approaching her, but the teacher enters, and the opportunity is gone.

One hour of English leaves me bleary eyed and exhausted. As I hear the bell announcing the end of the day, I feel relieved. The first one to leave is Coral, who dashes outside. I grab my bag and run after her.

"Coral!" I call her. She ignores me, and runs into the bathroom. I sigh, and with a deep sense of déjàvu I sit on the bench nearby. I wait patiently, glancing at my watch every couple of minutes. After a while I realize I've missed the school bus. I am walking home today. I wait on.

Twenty minutes later Coral comes out. She definitely cried in there and did a terrible job of hiding it. I wonder if I looked the same when our roles were reversed.

"I'm sorry," I say. "I didn't mean to hurt you."

"I think you actually did mean to," she answers.

I mull over it for a second. "Maybe. A bit. I'm still sorry. You're not a coward at all."

"Yes, I am. You were right. I'm always afraid that the teachers will yell at me."

"You aren't a coward where it matters."

"Fine," she sniffs. "We've missed the school bus."

"Yes. Let's walk."

On the way home I tell her about the phone call I made. She seems to be as shocked as I am. "But we just talked to her yesterday," she says.

"We talked to someone yesterday," I correct her.

"Are you sure the woman you talked to wasn't Patricia?"

"She sounded completely different. Anyway, why would she say that she's dead?"

"It's really weird."

"Yes," I agree. "So what now?"

"I don't know. I need to think about it," she says. "My house is here."

I look at the house she's pointing at. It's not a house at all. It's a palace.

"Wow," I say. "Are your parents movie stars or something?"

She fidgets uncomfortably. "No. My dad's a lawyer. He's just pretty successful."

"Nice. Maybe I should be a lawyer too."

"Well, you still have some time before you need to make decisions about your professional future," she reminds me. "Let's talk later."

I nod and we say goodbye. I walk on. Near my home I spot Peter, walking vigorously.

"Hey!" I say. "What's up?"

He smiles. "Amy! How are you feeling?"

"I don't know. Fine, I guess."

"But are you still sick?"

"What? No, I'm not sick."

"Oh… okay." He looks embarrassed.

We both stand and look at each other. Come on, Amy, say something, say something, this silence is becoming uncomfortable…

"You're a student at Sunset Ridge, right?" says Peter.

"That's right."

"Yeah. My sister goes to your school. Her name is Carley."

"Oh, really?" Damn it. Carley. So that's how everyone knew that I called him that night. What a bitch…

"Whistling still bothering you at night?" he interrupts my line of thought.

"Oh no, that stopped completely," I lie, wishing to avoid the subject. "Say... did you ever hear about Kimberly White?"

He furrows his brow. "Kimberly White? From Washington Street? The girl who disappeared?"

"Yeah."

"Sure. It was a big story when I was a kid here."

"You grew up here?"

"Yeah, I lived just next to your school. So, what about Kimberly White?"

"I don't know. It's a sad story."

He nods. "Yeah. Most people think she got a ride with someone she shouldn't have. Her mother tried to convince the cops to keep on searching, but... I don't know. I guess they just didn't find anything."

"And what happened to her parents?"

"Her father died when she was a little girl. Her mother died a few years after Kimberly disappeared. Where did you find out about this story, anyway?"

"I heard it at school."

"Good. I'm glad they're talking about it. There's a good reason that I was worried when I saw you walking around in the middle of the night."

"I guess you're right."

"I am. Well, I have to carry on with my patrol..."

"No problem. Peter?"

"What?"

"What would you do if you knew that Kimberly had been kidnapped?"

"I'm actually pretty sure she was kidnapped," he answers seriously. "She disappeared without a trace... Why? Did you hear something?"

"No. Just... you know."

"See you, Amy."

"Bye."

I unlock the front door. There is no one home. I go to my room, open my laptop and browse to the Google Maps page. I look for Washington Street in Narrowdale. I then look for Oak Street. The woman claiming to be Patricia White said that Kimberly was leaving her friend's house at Oak Street. Any reasonable way from Oak Street to Washington Street goes through two streets I know well. Weldon Avenue is the street where we heard the scream. Maple Street is where I live.

I glance out my window at Alex's house. What if he saw Kimberly walking by his house? Perhaps he was waiting for her outside? What if Kimberly's kidnapper is living next to me? He had already threatened me twice to stop investigating her disappearance, after all. What if...?

My cell rings, making me leap three feet into the air in fright. This stress is really bad for me.

"Amy?"

"Hey, Coral."

"Listen, I found another article about Kimberly White in an archive of the local newspaper online."

"Anything interesting?"

"No, just another article asking for anyone with information to call the police, but there's a picture of Patricia here."

"What's the link?"

"It's long. I'll message it to you."

I wait impatiently.

"Sent," she announces a few seconds later.

I open the new message from Coral. It has only a link and I click it. A second later, the article appears on the screen, along with the picture.

"That's the woman who talked to us," I say, my voice quavering.

"Yes. So the woman you talked to lied to you."

"But I just talked to Peter, from security. He said that she died a couple of years after Kimberly disappeared."

"Amy, we have pictures of us talking to this woman!"

"Only in Narrowdale," I mumble.

"What?"

"Feel like dropping by her place again?"

"I don't know," she hesitates. "Okay. Sure. There must be a rational explanation for all of this."

I am actually pretty sure that the explanation is not rational at all, but we agree to meet near the Whites' house at five thirty, and I hang up.

CHAPTER TWENTY-NINE

I arrive to Patricia White's home and look around. Coral is nowhere to be seen. I pull out my phone and glance at it. It's a quarter past four! Why did I get here so early? What should I do until Coral shows up?

My feet start walking, taking me towards the mall. I try telling myself I'm just going to buy myself something to eat until Coral shows up. I've barely touched my lunch. I must be starving.

Yeah, right. Who am I trying to fool?

I find him sitting in the shade, leaning against one of the mall's walls. He doesn't budge as I come closer. Only his eyes seem to follow my movement.

"Hi, Edgar," I say.

"You shouldn't be here," he says lazily. "You have somewhere else to be."

"I have some time," I say. I rummage in my pocket. "I have some money. Do you want something to eat?"

"Another time, maybe." He shuts his eyes. "I'm tired."

I pull my hand out of my pocket in surprise. "You don't want any money?"

He doesn't answer.

"Edgar, I wanted to ask. Kimberly White... Why is it me who is dreaming about her?"

"Who?"

"Kimberly. The one that you've told us about. From nine and a half years ago."

"You dream about someone I talked about nine and a half years ago?"

"What? No, I mean–" I stop, confused. "We spoke about her two days ago, remember? I was here with my friends…"

"Sometimes it's so hard to concentrate," says Edgar. "And I really am trying to rest. It's not polite to intrude on someone's nap."

"I just want to know why it is me who's dreaming about her, and not someone else."

"Who says someone else is not dreaming about her?" asks Edgar. "Maybe other people are dreaming about her as well."

I stare at him, stunned.

"Maybe all of the women in Narrowdale are dreaming the same dream every night." He laughs "That could be interesting."

"But…"

"I want to dream as well," he says drowsily. "But someone is bothering me."

"It's not anyone else and you know it," I say angrily. "It's only me! Why me?"

"Your… surrounding thing is similar," he says, irritated. "It really is very similar. Extraordinary."

"What?" I have no idea what he's talking about.

"Your surrounding thing. Your flavor. Your climate. You know what I'm talking about!" He opens his eyes and stands up abruptly. He lifts his hands and waves them around my head. "The thing around you. It's really similar to hers."

"What do you mean? I don't understand…"

"Listen well," he says, his eyes unusually sharp. "I will only say this once."

"Okay," I say, clenching my fists in suspense.

"I Am Really Tired," he says, emphasizing each word. "I like to nap during the afternoon. You are bothering me, and I don't like it. Have a nice day." He sits down, turns his back to me and starts snoring.

"Edgar?"

He snores a ridiculously loud and unconvincing snore.

Apparently, our talk is over. I walk back to Patricia White's house.

CHAPTER THIRTY

At a quarter past five Coral appears down the street, riding her bike. I wave at her.

"You're early." I smile.

"You too."

"Yeah. I... I just went over to the mall to see Edgar."

"Really?" Coral's eyes widen in surprise. "What did he say?"

"Nothing that made any sense. Say..." I hesitate. "Coral, do you sometimes see things in Narrowdale that other people don't?"

For a moment there's something in her eyes. A spark of an old memory, perhaps? It quickly disappears.

"No, what do you mean?" she asks. "What sort of things?"

"I don't know, forget it," I say. "It's just something that Shane said."

"I don't recall ever seeing anything unusual. At least...," she adds with a half smile, "not until you got here."

"Well, thanks a lot."

"Don't mention it."

"Okay," I sigh. "now what?"

She looks at the house for a second. "I think we should knock on her door."

"And what if the woman who called herself Patricia opens the door?"

"I don't know."

"And what if the other one opens the door?"

"Well, then we will... I don't know."

"Coral, that's the best plan ever."

"Do you have a better plan?"

I ponder this. "Actually... no."

We approach the front door.

"Right," says Coral. "Let's do it."

I knock on the door. "One second!" I hear a voice from inside, and I instantly recognize it as the woman who spoke to me on the phone. A second later she opens the door. She's dark-haired, about thirty, wearing leggings and a faded T-shirt, and looks pregnant.

"Hi," she says. "Can I help you?"

We stand and stare.

"Yes?" she asks impatiently.

"We're... fundraising!" I blurt out. "We're collecting money for cancer."

"You're fundraising for cancer?" She frowns.

"Yes. I mean, no! Of course not. We're totally against cancer. We're fundraising for..."

"For patients in the children's hospital." Coral saves me. "In the cancer ward. We wanted to know if you want to donate some money."

"I usually don't donate for door-to-door fundraising," she answers. "Do you have a permit for fundraising?"

Fundraising needs a permit? Oh dear.

"Of course we do," says Coral smoothly. "We're registered at the city council. You can check."

I stare at her open mouthed. We're registered?

"Okay, but don't you have any brochure or printout to show me?"

"Oh, no," Coral continues. "They didn't give us anything."

"Well, I'm sorry; I'm not really comfortable with donating for door-to-door fundraising anyway."

"Maybe someone else at your home—" I start to say.

"There's no one else here," she cuts me off coldly. "And I don't want to donate."

"Mommy, who is it?" I hear a small boy from inside.

"Just some girls fundraising, honey," she answers.

"Well, thank you very much," I say.

"I donate annually in church for cancer patients," the woman says. "Have a nice day."

The door closes. We walk away.

"That went well," I say. "Now what?"

"Where is the woman who talked to us last time?" asks Coral. "Where's Patricia?"

"Patricia is dead."

"So who opened the door for us?"

"I don't know. Now what?"

"Maybe we should go home," she suggests. "I have to babysit Mia today."

"Okay." I glance at my watch. "What time do you have to be back?"

"Seven."

"Coral, it's only half past five! We have plenty of time!"

"I just don't want to be late."

"Maybe we should try peeking inside," I suggest. "We might see Patricia. She was older. Maybe she's this woman's mother."

"Well… why would she lie?"

"I have no idea, but it makes more sense than the alternative. Come on, let's check it out."

"Okay, but after that we'll split, because I have to be home by seven."

"You'll make it, don't worry." I look around. "You can climb that tree over there. You'll probably be able to see over the fence into the house from there."

"*I* can climb?" Coral says disbelievingly. "Why should I be the one climbing?"

"'Cause you're a village girl. You've spent your entire childhood running in the fields and climbing trees. You probably walked barefoot all the time and… played with rabbits and squirrels."

"My childhood sounds fascinating. I've never climbed a tree in my life, and I'm not about to start now."

"Coral, just listen. This shirt is one of my favorite shirts and if I tear it–"

"Amy, I'm not going to climb that tree. I'll fall down!"

"Why would you? It has lots and lots of branches. I'm wearing platform shoes–"

"Then let's both not climb that tree. What kind of an idea is that, anyway?"

I sigh. "Fine, I'll climb that tree, but if I rip my shirt on one of the branches, it's all your fault."

"Sure. My fault. Crazy girl."

I approach the tree. The truth is I haven't climbed many trees in my life either, and every time I did climb one, I had my father helping me. Never mind, how complicated can it be? A foot here, now there's a bump in the trunk over there, this foot goes on the branch over here... this is just like climbing a ladder! Left foot on that branch over th–

The branch breaks, and I'm hanging for my life.

"Amy, is everything all right?" Coral whispers.

"I am about to die. Call the fire department."

"You're just two feet high. You can jump down."

"I'll break my legs."

"You won't even scratch your knee. I told you climbing the tree was a bad idea."

I ignore her, and swing my legs towards the trunk. I manage to grab a thick branch with my right leg and slowly pull myself towards it. I hug the trunk, trying to calm my beating heart. I've reached this far; I can finish what I've started. What did we learn, Amy? Do not step on thin, dry branches. Right.

Another foot, now hold the branch over there, pull myself up, I can practically sit here...

"Wow, Amy, you're kind of high. Perhaps you should stop there."

I look down, and instantly regret it. Apparently, I'm half a mile above the ground. This tree is way higher than I thought, and it's swinging in the wind! I hug it tightly and shut my eyes.

"Amy?"

"What?"

"Isn't it hard to look inside the house with your eyes shut?"

"No, no, I got this."

"'Cause when I close my eyes, I see mostly darkness."

"Yeah?"

"Maybe with you it's different."

"Yeah. Just give me a second."

"Okay, but I have to go home soon. I have to take care of Mia."

"Coral," I beg her. "Please be quiet."

She finally shuts up. I slowly open my eyes and attempt to look around me without looking down. There's that woman's house… It's a bit hard to see through those windows. I can spot some children's toys scattered in the yard, and I can definitely see the porch that we sat on. Wow, this tree is swinging. Where's all this wind coming from? It's the end of the summer! I close my eyes, take deep breaths. You won't fall Amy; you're holding tight, and this tree's been here for a while. It isn't about to collapse. I open my eyes again and focus on one of the windows. I think it's the kitchen window. It's hard to see. Perhaps if I just move my head a bit… Yes! There's another window, just next to the neighbor's garden, the one with the scarecrow.

My hands are grasping at dirt. He's pulling me back inside and I try to hold on to something, anything, to pull myself outside, and the scarecrow standing in the garden seems as if it is mocking my attempts to escape…

"Amy!!!"

I open my eyes wide and scream. For some reason, I've let the trunk go, and I'm falling backwards, my arms flailing around, trying to catch one of the branches around me. One hand is left holding a bunch of leaves, and the other manages to grasp a small, green branch, which I'm certain will break… but it holds.

"Amy, are you all right?"

"Hang on." I slowly and carefully pull myself back to the trunk and hug it tightly.

"Maybe you should get down."

"I'm not sure I know how to."

"Why did you let go? You nearly fell!"

"I think I saw… something." Stupidly I glance at the neighbor's garden once more. There it is. The scarecrow. It seems shabbier, and its shirt is completely torn, but it is the same scarecrow, the one I saw in my dream.

"I think I want to get down."

"Good."

"Get a ladder."

"What? Where do you want me to get a ladder from? Just go down the same way you got up!"

"I can't."

"Why not?"

"Because I can't."

"There, the branch you climbed before is just next to your right foot."

"No, I can't."

"Amy."

"I can't."

She sighs. "Do you want me to go to that woman's house and ask for a ladder?"

"Are you nuts? She'll think I climbed the tree to peek into her house!"

"But you did climb the tree to peek into her house."

"Coral, don't."

"I can go to someone else here–"

"No!!!" I scream hysterically. "Coral, do not go to anyone's house in this street!"

"What? Why?"

"Because… Trust me. Just don't. I can handle this, I'm coming down."

Okay, one foot fumbles around. The branch is here, I know it is. I'll just look down… That was a mistake. Here's the branch. Now the second foot, but what should I do with this hand here? Perhaps it should go over there? This position is not ideal. Now how can I lower the other foot? I'll fall! I have to let go with this hand. I'm about to die. Why did I wear platform shoes? Why did I climb this stupid tree? Why did we move to Narrowdale? Ground! I've reached ground!

I lie down on the dirt in utter relief.

"Your favorite shirt is dirty," remarks Coral. "I told you it was stupid."

"Thank you, Coral, for the support. Yes, I'm fine, don't worry about me." I'm breathing hard as if I ran ten miles.

"So you saw something?"

"Yes." I get up. "But not in her house."

"What? So what did you see?"

"Last time I dreamt I nearly escaped."

"I know, you mentioned that," she says sharply, probably recalling our argument.

"When I was escaping, I saw a garden. A garden and a scarecrow. Coral, that neighbor's back yard over there has the same scarecrow."

"Are you sure... What–"

"I think the man who kidnapped Kimberly was her neighbor, and I think he's holding her in his house, this house."

"But Amy–"

"And he's still holding her," I go on, cutting off her words. "She's still there!"

"What? Nine and a half years?"

"Maybe." I grab her hand. "Coral, we have to find out."

"Amy, this is a very bad idea..."

"She might be alive!"

"Someone would have heard her call for help. She would have managed to escape..."

"No! He had her tied and gagged!"

"Amy!" she says. "No one could live like that for nine and a half years. Even if he did hold her there at the beginning, he probably moved her or..." She stops and doesn't say what's on both our minds.

"You're probably right," I agree reluctantly. "But still, I have to see if she's still there!"

"Fine," she says. "Then let's call the police."

"And tell them what? That I dreamt I know where Kimberly's kidnapper is? That we talked to her mother, who died seven years ago? We have to get something more solid."

"Like what?"

"We need to get into the house with the scarecrow."

"Hang on!" she stops me. "Not again. We are not about to knock on his door and tell him that we're fundraising for cancer. And we're definitely not about to knock on his door and ask him about Kimberly White."

"Agreed," I say. "So what do you suggest?"

"I suggest thinking about it before we do something stupid. If he really is the person who kidnapped Kimberly White, we should snoop around a bit."

"Snoop?"

"Yes, snoop. Do you have a problem with my vocabulary?"

"No, no, it's great. Let's 'snoop.'"

Coral and I approach the gate of the front yard and peer at the house. The entire house looks old, and in bad shape. The paint is dry and peeling at points. Despite the scarecrow, there are no plants or flowers in the yard, only weeds and dirt. The scarecrow, a faceless wooden pole with some ancient dirty clothes, looks as if it might collapse any second. I doubt it actually scares any birds, but it creeps the hell out of me.

"There's a sign on the door," she whispers. "Can you see what's written on it?"

I look beyond the unkempt yard at the front door. "Hang on…" I squint. "Tom Ellis… or it might be Tony Ellis…"

"So what is it, Tony or Tom?"

"I don't know, it's really hard to see from here."

She points to the pickup truck parked in the street next to the house. "I think he's at home right now."

"Or he might have gone somewhere by foot, or on a bike," I suggest.

She walks over to the truck and looks inside the window. "Tom Ellis. His car's papers are on the passenger seat."

"He seems to be living alone," I say. "There's only one name on the door."

"Yeah, and his yard is a complete disaster," says Coral. "Everything's yellow and dry."

"Okay, now what?"

She looks at her watch. "I have to go home."

"You have plenty of time."

"I don't want to be late."

"Fine." I sigh. "Go home."

She looks at me suspiciously. "You aren't going to do anything stupid, right?"

"Why would I do anything stupid?" I ask, annoyed.

"You're making that face that you make... Could you wait? I want to research Tom Ellis before you do something stupid."

"Fine, check him out. I won't do anything stupid before you let me know what you find out."

"Thanks." She gets on her bike. "Do you want a ride?"

"On your bike? No, thanks. Besides, your house is the opposite way from mine."

"Amy, don't do anything stupid."

"Okay, okay."

She smiles and rides away. I start walking home, deep in thoughts. Tonight I'm about to do something really stupid.

CHAPTER THIRTY-ONE

I have no appetite during dinner. I toy a little with the scrambled eggs that Mom made. I add some cream cheese to the eggs and stir them together, creating an unappetizing sludge, from which I force myself to take a bite. I need lots of energy tonight.

"Amy, I'll take you tomorrow afternoon. We'll leave at about four, okay?" Mom smiles at me.

"Leave?" I look at her in confusion.

"To Nicole's. Aren't you staying at her place this weekend?"

"Oh, right. Yes… I guess." I eat some dry toast. What a banquet.

"Amy, I need to know for sure if you're going." Mom furrows her brow. "I want to plan my weekend."

"Yeah, sure, I'm going to Nicole's. Absolutely."

"Okay. Tomorrow at four?"

"Great. Thanks, Mom, I'm done eating." I take my dish to the sink and go to my room.

My phone rings. It's Shane.

"Hey, Shane."

"Amy? Coral said that you know who kidnapped Kimberly White."

"That's right. His name is Tom Ellis. He was her neighbor."

"She also said that you're about to do something stupid."

"Why would she think that?" I ask, irritated. "I promised I wouldn't."

"Amy."

"What?"

"Are you planning on doing something stupid?"

"I'm about to break into his house tonight."

Silence. "Amy, this isn't funny."

"Tell me about it."

"Amy…"

"Shane, she could still be there! He might be keeping her in his basement…"

"You sound insane."

"And even if she isn't there, I have to prove it's him!"

"Amy, you can't just break into someone's house!"

"It's not 'someone.' It's the bastard who kidnapped Kimberly…"

"So you think."

"So I know! Don't you start! It's him!"

"Fine, fine," he placates me. "Then call the police."

"Sure. What should I tell them first? About the dead woman who gave us water? About the time I was possessed in your room? About the all-knowing homeless man? Oh yeah, me and the cops, we'll have a great chat!"

"Amy."

"Shane, I'm going."

"Fine, but when?"

"Tonight."

"What time?"

"What difference does it make?"

"I'm coming with you."

"The hell you are," I say angrily. "You're staying home. This is dangerous!"

"Then don't do it."

"I have to."

"Then so do I. I won't let you go alone."

"Shane, stop being an idiot. You've known me for only a week, and suddenly you're my best friend? Chill, okay? I'm not about to drag you into this."

"You already have," he says calmly. "And it's true, I've only known you for a week, but I won't let you risk your life without helping out. If this is the guy who kidnapped Kimberly White, he's dangerous."

"Exactly!" I say victoriously. "Which is why–"

"Which is why I'm coming. What time?"

I groan. "Be at Tom Ellis's place at one."

"Where's that?"

"It's the house to the right of Patricia's... of what used to be Patricia's home."

"Cool. See you there."

"And don't tell Coral anything."

"See you at one." He hangs up.

I put my phone down, troubled. Now I'm endangering someone else with my bullshit. Maybe I should just let it go...? No. I recall the feeling of him dragging me... her into the house. If Kimberly's there, I have to save her, and if she isn't... I have to prove that he kidnapped her. Tom Ellis will pay for what he did.

But what if something happens? I need to prepare, but how can I prepare for something like that?

I pace around my room, restless. A strange idea comes to me, and I contemplate it for a while. Finally, I pick up my phone and dial.

"Honey!!!" Nicole screeches at me.

"Hey, Nicky, what's up?"

"Fantastic! Guess what happened today at school?"

I cannot guess. She starts telling me a long tale about someone who sent her a note, and the teacher caught her, or maybe the teacher sent her the note, possibly it was someone who sent the teacher a note, I am entirely unsure, unable to concentrate. Finally I say, "Nicole, that's the most incredible thing I've ever heard, but listen for a sec–I have a favor to ask."

"Is it about tomorrow?"

"What? No."

"You're still coming, right?"

"Yeah, but never mind that. Look, tonight I... I'm about to do something a bit dangerous. I need your help."

"What? What are you going to do?"

"Never mind what. I'm about to live stream a video at night. The video will upload as I am filming it."

"What's dangerous about that? Are you worried that my computer will catch a virus because of it?"

"No!" Nicole's grasp of technology is underwhelming. "Of course not! What I'll do while filming is a bit… I need you to watch the video as I stream it, and if you see anything bad happening, I want you to call someone."

"Something bad? Honey!" She sounds stressed. "What are you about to do?"

"Never mind. If something bad happens I want you to call Peter. I'll give you his number. Are you writing this down?"

"Hang on, I'll get some paper."

I patiently wait until she finds something to write on, and dictate his phone number. Then I give her Tom Ellis's address.

"Tell him that's where I went, and that I need help. And let him know what you saw in the video."

"Honey…" She starts crying. "You're scaring me. Maybe we should talk about it tomorrow, at my place instead?"

"Nicole, I really need your help. And don't tell the Jennifers. They'll just panic."

"Right, 'cause I'm so cool and relaxed right now."

"Nicole, you're my hero."

"Honey… Don't do anything stupid."

"Me? Stupid? Of course not."

I hang up. Well, it's sort of a plan. I just hope she won't ruin it all.

CHAPTER THIRTY-TWO

I walk down the dark street. My hands are shoved deep down my pockets, and my heart is pounding. Shadows of houses and trees darken the surroundings, making every murky shape suspicious, every corner threatening. In the distance, a dog is howling a long, desperate howl. I shudder, my breath short and panicky. I look around me. Is there anyone else here?

Yes, someone is following me, I'm almost sure of it. I hold my breath, fighting my reflexes which scream at me to run, to shout, to escape. There it is again. Footsteps, getting closer. I freeze. A strange hand grabs my shoulder, and I whirl, a scream running up my throat...

"Amy, are you all right?" Shane asks, looking worried.

"Yes, it's just–" I take a deep breath. "Everything's scarier at night. And we agreed that you'd wait next to Tom's house!"

"We did." He nods. "But I didn't want you walking on your own in the middle of the night."

"Okay." I seem to run out of things to say. I inspect him. He's wearing dark clothes, his camera hanging on his shoulder. He looks the same as I do. Scared.

"Shall we?" he asks.

"Yeah. Let's go."

We start walking towards Tom Ellis's house. We both wear sneakers, and you can hardly hear our footsteps in the silent night, but I could swear that my heartbeat can be heard a mile away.

"Did you bring your laptop?" Shane asks me.

"Yeah."

"So what exactly is our plan?" he asks.

"You'll put my backpack with the laptop on your back. We hook it up to the camera and upload the video to my blog while filming it. I have a friend watching at home. If… If anything happens, she'll call for help."

"Okay. Are you sure you know how to upload a video like that?"

"I watched a video online. It doesn't look complicated. It should work," I answer.

We walk silently for a couple of minutes.

"What if the help won't get there in time?" Shane asks.

"Let's hope it does. Better yet, let's hope we don't need it."

"What if there's a burglar alarm?"

"Let's hope there's no burglar alarm."

We halt in front of Tom's house.

"You can still change your mind," I tell Shane. "It's not too late."

"Give me the backpack," he answers.

I take the backpack off, pull out my laptop and turn it on. We connect Shane's camera, making sure that the laptop is receiving its output. I activate the program that's supposed to upload the video to the blog. I've already configured it at home, so all I have to do is press "start."

"Wait!" a voice calls behind us. I nearly piss my pants.

"Wait for me!" Coral swerves her bicycle and stops next to us, her breaks squealing.

"What are you doing here?" I whisper, hoping that no one heard the noise she was making.

"Shane said you're about to break into Tom's house!"

"I told you not to tell her!" I hiss at him angrily.

"Yup, you did."

"Coral, it's too dangerous…"

"Amy, I'm not here to argue," she says resolutely. "I'm part of this. I'm not about to let you do this on your own."

I look at her, consider refusing, even cancelling the whole thing. Instead I feel tears of gratitude in my eyes, and I stay silent. What exactly made those two help me? How long have we known each other? Two weeks? And already they're willing to risk their lives like that?

"Coral... Shane... I just want to say..."

Coral lays her hand on my arm. "No problem. Let's get this over with."

I nod and look at them both. "Thanks."

We stand quietly, looking at each other for another minute. Then I shut the laptop screen, putting it back in the backpack so that only the cable connected to the camera pokes out.

"Okay," I say hoarsely. "You can put the backpack on your back."

Shane puts the backpack on his back. I send a short message to Nicole with the link to the video page in my blog, my fingers shaking the entire time.

CHAPTER THIRTY-THREE

It feels almost as if someone turned off the streetlights when we walk into Tom Ellis's yard. The darkness is like a heavy weight draped all over me, slowing my movements, crushing me down. Nearly nothing grows in his yard. Just weeds and strange dead twisted branches that were probably once bushes, but have been stripped clean of all their leaves. In the middle of the yard stands a scarecrow. The scarecrow.

The top half of my body is outside the window. I can see a small vegetable garden, a scarecrow standing in the middle, flowers all around... I hear the door behind me fling open. He is shouting, but I can't understand what he's saying...

I breathe slowly. No vegetables now. No flowers. Just the scarecrow, its clothes worn and torn by the years.

I point at the closest window. "I think we can start by checking windows."

"What if he has a burglar alarm?" Coral asks.

"Let's hope he doesn't have a burglar alarm," I answer.

I approach the window and peer inside. A kitchen. I can spot some dirty dishes in the sink. The rest of the room is too dark to see. I try to open it, but it's definitely locked. I motion at Shane and Coral to move on. Shane nods, his camera pointed at me, faithfully recording everything. Is Nicole watching this right now? Is she freaking out, calling the police and my parents? Let's hope not.

I approach another window, then pause.

The window next to it pulls me closer with invisible strings. We've met before, it seems to say. And we have.

My hand touches something cold and smooth–glass. This is a window! I find the handle, turning it slowly. It's stuck, and I twist it harder. The window opens with a horrible screeching sound...

"There." I whisper. "I think this is the window that Kimberly tried to escape through."

Coral says something. She feels so far away, it's hard to hear her voice. I approach the window, my fear dissipating. This is right. This is where I'm supposed to be. I grasp the window and try to open it. It moves a bit. Not locked, just a bit stuck. I pull harder and it opens, emitting a loud squeak. We all crouch down.

"You think he heard that?" I can hear Shane saying. So far. He's just so far.

"I don't know," I answer distantly. "Let's wait a bit."

We wait in the darkness. The seconds crawl. It's becoming harder and harder to concentrate. Why am I here? To find Kimberly. She was taken...

No. You are Kimberly.

No. Kimberly disappeared a long time ago. She was kidnapped by Tom Ellis.

You were kidnapped. He took you to his home. Why did you come back?

I... I didn't, I just want to help her...

There is no one to help. Get out of here, Kimberly, before it's too late.

No. I'm... I'm... Amy.

"I think we're good," I say, my mind foggy. "Let's go inside."

I stand up and approach the window. Coral is saying something. Why is she here? Why am I here? I climb up the window, drop down, look around. I can hear Shane outside saying, "Hang on, what's that?" but it doesn't matter. Only this room matters. She was here...

I was here.

This is where he kept her...

This is where he kept me.

"Amy!" someone is shouting outside. Who's Amy? There is no one in this room. I am too late. Too late for what? Why did I return here? This is where he kept me…

"Amy, get out of there!"

"Amy, someone's coming!"

The light turns on, and I see him. And I scream.

CHAPTER THIRTY-FOUR

He stares at me, and my vision suddenly blurs…

It's spring. I'm seventeen, reading a book on the front porch. The book is boring, something I have to finish up for school, and I skip over the really tedious parts. I lift my eyes, and notice our neighbor in his yard. He looks as if he went out to tend his garden, but he's just standing there, doing nothing, scrutinizing me. It makes me feel uncomfortable, and I walk inside, closing the door behind me.

Middle of the night. I'm hot. I'm lying in bed, a fan aimed straight at me, but I can't fall asleep. It's July, the whole room is buzzing with mosquitoes, and I'm sweating. I turn the light on and approach my window. As I open it, I notice Tom Ellis, the neighbor. He is standing by his front door, his eyes staring in my direction. I back away and turn off the light. I have a very hard time falling asleep.

Winter time. I'm just coming back from college, trudging from the bus station. It's raining, and despite my coat I'm getting wet. Soon I'll be home. Maybe Mom will make me some soup… A car stops by me. It's our neighbor, Tom.

"Kimberly!" he says. "Hop in, I'll take you home!"

"No, thanks," I quickly say.

"What? Why not? You're soaking wet!"

"Yes, but I'm not on my way home," I lie. "I'm going to my friend's house, and she lives right here." I point to the house behind me.

He looks at me, and his eyes suddenly narrow in anger. "No problem," he snarls. "Have a nice day." He closes his window, and hits the gas. His car squeals away, frighteningly fast. I breathe out in relief, waiting in the rain for a couple of moments, making sure he's not coming back. I should talk to Mom about him.

Thanksgiving. Me and Billy are standing in the middle of the sidewalk, hugging. Tom Ellis is walking on the other side of the road. He stops and looks at us, saying nothing, just staring. I ignore him and we walk on. I can feel his eyes burrowing in my back. I am not a little girl anymore, and I'm not afraid of him.

I slowly return to my senses. I'm not Kimberly, I'm Amy. He's standing in front of me, Tom Ellis, looking nothing like a kidnapper. He's just an ordinary guy, a little fat, unshaved. He's wearing a dirty white T-shirt and shorts. His hair is black and cropped. He keeps asking me something, over and over.

"What are you doing here?"

"I'm not afraid of you," I blurt out. "Where's Kimberly?"

His eyes widen in terror and his mouth hangs open, but a second later he suddenly becomes calm, composed.

"I think you're mistaken," he says. "There's no Kimberly here."

"Oh, sorry," I quickly say. "My mistake. I thought this was my friend's house. I... I'll leave now." My eyes dart around, then suddenly meet his own.

His face changes completely. His look becomes warm, the angry lines in his forehead disappear, and he smiles a wide smile.

"Hey, sure," he says. "We all make mistakes."

"Yes, that's right," I say. "So... which way is the way out?"

"The front door is that way," he motions.

I start walking towards the doorway, my entire body shivering.

"Hang on," Tom says as I'm walking past him. "Did you mean Kimberly White?"

"What?" I say.

"Yeah." He nods. "She's right here."

"Kimberly White is here?" I ask in a choked voice.

"Sure. Come on, she's in the other room," he says. I walk in the direction he's pointing, leaving him behind me.

Something hits my head, and everything turns black.

CHAPTER THIRTY-FIVE

Whistling. The same jarring, terrible whistling. My head hurts, a dull, throbbing pain. My hands are tied behind my back. I can't move them at all. Something is stuffed in my mouth, gagging me. I slowly open my eyes and realize that this is not another dream.

I am lying on my back inside the same room that I broke into through the window. The same room that, nine and a half years ago, Kimberly was trapped in, tied up, bleeding. Tom Ellis is sitting in front of me on an old rickety stool, whistling a very familiar tune. As he sees me opening my eyes, he smiles, exposing yellow, crooked teeth.

"You're back," he says softly. "I was sure you'd never come back after what I did. But you knew it was all a mistake. I was just so angry…"

I stare at him fearfully. What is he talking about? Back from where? I have to get out of here. How long until Nicole calls Peter? How long until Coral and Shane call the police? How long do I have until someone gets here?

"You know," he says. "I thought a lot about that night. I simply can't understand what you tried to do. It seemed as if you were trying to leave! Why? We were finally together; it was perfect! What happened?"

I mumble something unintelligibly.

"Right," he says. "I'll get this rag out of your mouth. You won't scream, right? If you scream, someone might hear you. That would just complicate things, right?"

I nod. He leans over me and starts untying the rag tied around my mouth. His fingernails are disgustingly black, and he smells sour, like old salami that was left out of the fridge. Finally I feel my mouth coming free.

"Please..." I sob. "I made a mistake, I thought this was my friend's house..."

"A mistake? What are you talking about? Kimberly, everything's fine. You can relax, I know it's you, I–"

"I don't know what you're talking about. My name is not Kimberly, you've got the wrong person–"

"The wrong person? Don't you think I recognize your eyes? I can see them every time I go to sleep. It's been so many years, but I still know you..."

"I'm telling you, I'm not Kimberly. My name is Amy, I entered the wrong house–"

"No!" he shouts, agitated. "I... I know who you are! I would never forget, I..." He becomes silent and looks at me. "No. Of course. You're not Kimberly. Kimberly is a real woman, grown up. Not like you. You're just a kid. But those eyes! I was sure that..." He shakes his head, upset. "Who are you? How do you know about Kimberly White?"

"I just heard the name by chance. I don't know her at all."

He nods, gets up and rummages in a box on the far side of the room. When he comes back, I nearly scream. He's holding a rusty knife.

He kneels above me. "Who knows you're here?"

Peter, where are you? "No one! I swear! I thought this was my friend's house..."

He grabs me roughly and my head hits the floor. He holds the knife to my throat. It feels cold, and terribly sharp. I hold my breath.

"Do you always enter your friend's house through the window? How do you know Kimberly White?"

"I..."

Distantly, I hear loud thumping. He turns his head, moves the knife away. More thumping. A doorbell. Someone is knocking on his door. Peter?

"I'll be right back," he snarls, pushing the rag into my mouth. He leaves the room, and I can hear him locking the door behind him.

A small tapping from above me draws my attention. I lift my head painfully. It's Coral, by the window, trying to open it, but it's closed and locked now. She can't do it. I sob in despair as she walks away. I have to get out of here before he comes back!

Crash. A huge rock lands on the floor next to my head. Coral must have broken the window with it. She thrusts her hand through the broken glass and unlatches the window from inside. Within seconds she's by my side, pulling the rag out of my mouth.

"Coral, call the police, he's coming back!" I say shakily.

"By the time the police will get here, he'll kill you," she mutters, grabbing the knife from the floor.

"But he's–"

"I'm hoping Shane can buy us some time," she says, sawing at the rope around my hands.

"Shane?"

"He's the one knocking on the front door. Tom Ellis was chasing him down the street as I was breaking the window."

"If he catches him…"

She cuts my hands free, moves on to the legs. "Let's hope he doesn't."

"You're bleeding!" I say, noticing blood running down her arm.

"I cut myself on the window, it's nothing." She manages to free my legs. "Let's get out of here."

She leaps to her feet and climbs out through the window. I get up. My head is throbbing, and I force myself to shuffle forward. Footsteps behind me. I climb through the window, pulling myself out. The door opens behind me, and I hear him roaring.

A hand grabs my leg. I scream and attempt to shake it loose. He is pulling me back… My hands flail, trying to grab at something, anything at all…They grab Coral's outstretched hand.

"Coral, pull!" I scream. She pulls hard. Tom Ellis is pulling me from inside, they are stretching me painfully… I kick with my free leg, hitting something that seems to crunch. He yells in pain, and his grasp loosens. Coral heaves, and I fall on the ground. Outside.

"Run!" Coral shouts, and starts running. I get up and start running as well, but my head hurts, my vision is blurry. I trip. Tom Ellis is out the window, running after me, swinging something. A shovel? I get up, stumble forward. He's getting closer; he's right behind me... And then he shouts and falls.

I glance backwards. Tom Ellis is rolling on the ground fighting something that's growling and barking... A dog? It doesn't matter. I run, leaving the front yard. Coral's waiting outside on her bike. I sit behind her and hug her body.

"Coral, go, go!" I cry. The bike wobbles forward. Behind me I can hear Tom Ellis hollering. He's still after us!

"Coral, faster!"

She says nothing, her face tight with effort.

My head is about to explode. What's that terrible sound? What are those lights? Why is Coral stopping? I can't understand.

"Coral," I mumble. "Go. Faster."

"It's okay, Amy, we're okay," she says. "It's the police."

"What?" I'm confused. I stare at the lights. Red. Blue. A police car? The door opens and someone's getting out. Peter?

For the second time in one night, everything turns black.

CHAPTER THIRTY-SIX

A mild concussion, that's what the doctors say. I'll be fine; I simply need to rest, drink a lot of water, and avoid stress. In a couple of weeks I should be all better. For now, I still have headaches and dizzy spells, and there's nothing mild about it.

The nightmares stopped. At first I thought it was because of the sedatives I received in the hospital. But night after night I slept, and no dreams came. No whistling woke me up.

Mom and Dad asked a lot of questions at first. What was I doing out in the middle of the night? Why was I in Washington Street? What were Coral and Shane doing there? Who called the security guy? Who called the police?

I had a hard time answering, and once they saw it was causing me a lot of stress (No stress! No!), they let me be. Doubtless I'll have a lot to answer for in the near future, but for now I'm enjoying my small respite.

To help me avoid stress and to rest, they don't let my friends visit me. There's a whole discussion about bad influences which is also postponed until I feel better. They took my phone. When Mom caught me emailing Coral, my laptop was taken as well. Doctor's orders, of course.

Mom and Dad told me that Tom Ellis was arrested and is in jail, where he can't hurt me. However, they avoid divulging any other details. As far as I could piece it together from the short e-mails Coral sent me before my laptop was taken, the police charged Tom Ellis with assault. The arrest enabled them to search his house. Coral didn't know what they found, but his house was surrounded by cops, and there was no way to get close. She couldn't tell me if there was any sign of Kimberly.

There were additional things that she could not explain. Tom Ellis's leg was bleeding when they arrested him, and he was limping. It seemed as if something bit him. She didn't know what Peter told the cops, and she didn't know if Nicole or Peter informed the cops about the video on my blog. Just to be sure, I removed it from the blog as soon as I could.

Anthony has been driving me insane. He came back home as soon as he heard, and he's been sitting in my room for hours every day. If I kick him out he walks away, but comes back ten minutes later, like an irritating fly. Most of the time he doesn't even talk, just sits here. Sometimes he brings me things to eat, or drink, though I never ask for them, and I always snap at him when he does that.

Someone knocks on my door.

"Yes?" I say.

"Amy," says my Mom. "Can I come in?"

"Sure."

She opens the door and looks at me with a worried frown. I guess the bandages on my head scare her.

"How are you feeling?"

"I feel wonderful. It's almost as if I can see people, use my phone and surf the net."

"Just a little bit more, sweetie. The doctor said—"

"The doctor is an impostor. I bet he got his diploma in a cereal box. No stress? Boredom causes stress."

"There's someone here to see you."

I raise an eyebrow. My friends have been here at least a hundred times, and Mom has never let them through the front door.

"Yes?" I ask patiently.

"It's the security guy who… found you and helped you."

"Peter?"

"I think that's his name, yes."

"Can you please let him in?"

"Amy, if you're feeling tired, or your head is—"

"Mom, please let me talk to him for a couple of minutes." I turn my head towards Anthony, who is quietly sitting on the edge of my bed. "Shoo," I say.

"I'm really fine where I am right now," he answers.

"Go away. I want some peace and quiet."

"Then maybe you should tell the security guy that—"

"Mom! Get him out of here!"

They both leave the room. A second later Peter walks in, wearing his uniform. He seems much taller when I'm lying down in bed.

I wait. He doesn't say anything.

"What?" I finally ask.

"Your head…"

"My head is fine. The doctors promised that it won't fall off." He sits on my chair.

"Thanks for rescuing me." I smile at him.

"Amy, I didn't rescue you. The police did that. What… what were you thinking?"

I look at him silently.

"Why did you break into that guy's house? What made you think he had anything to do with Kimberly White? Why in God's name didn't you tell me or the police about your suspicions?"

"Because you wouldn't have believed me."

"Why not?"

I think about it. How do I explain it all? How do I talk about the last couple of weeks without sounding crazy?

"I think… I had nightmares. Nightmares in which I was kidnapped at night and taken to a dark room where I was tied up. I believe this is what happened to Kimberly nine and a half years ago."

Peter doesn't say anything, his mouth slightly open.

"There was whistling at night. I told you about that. The whistling was part of it. Tom Ellis whistled just like that before he kidnapped Kimberly. Those were the whistles that she heard that night. In some way I've experienced some of what she did."

"Amy…"

"In Tom Ellis's yard there was a scarecrow. I dreamt about that scarecrow…"

"Amy, that can't be."

I stop talking. This should have been the moment where I come clean and Peter understands what happens. When he realizes that Narrowdale is not what it seems to be, that there are shadows and mysteries lurking everywhere. And perhaps, to help him cope with the knowledge, to help me with the emotions that my confession brought up, we might kiss. Except… this isn't how things happen.

"You had strange dreams because you moved to a new place. You were under a lot of pressure," he says. "The whistling was just some guy. Maybe he even tried to harass you, I don't know. I told you, everything has a logical explanation."

I think about Patricia White, who talked to us seven years after she died, about Edgar, about the scream I heard in the middle of the night, a scream that Kimberly screamed a decade ago. I look at Peter, so convinced that he knows better. How will he explain it all? Everything has a logical explanation, if you try hard enough. "I guess you're right." I nod. "Did you tell the police? About my blog? That I broke into his house?"

"No." He shifts uncomfortably in his chair. "I told them that someone reported screaming from Tom Ellis's house."

"You lied?"

"Well, they're bound to find out eventually. For one, he'll probably tell them about it. Why did you tell your friend to call me? Why didn't you tell her to call the police immediately?" He looks pissed off.

"Because I knew you would do the right thing."

"I called the police!"

"See? I knew you would do the right thing."

"Amy…"

"And now Kimberly's kidnapper is behind bars. Isn't that a good thing?"

"How do you even know that he had anything to do with Kimberly?" he asks sharply.

My heart starts beating faster. "Did he?" I ask shakily. "Did… did they find her?"

"Amy…" His eyes become soft. "The police dogs found her… remains. Buried in the yard. Next to the scarecrow."

"I see," I say, my throat clenching.

"He probably killed her immediately after he kidnapped her."

"Not immediately." a tear rolls down my cheek. "It took a few days."

He looks at me, unsure what to say.

"Peter, my head hurts. I need to rest."

"Of course." He gets up from the chair. "I… I hope you feel better."

"Thanks," I say.

He leaves, closing the door behind him. I shut my eyes and weep silently for a very long time.

CHAPTER THIRTY-SEVEN

Kimberly was buried in the town's cemetery, next to her mother's grave. Today, after two weeks of being trapped at home, Mom finally lets me leave for a short while. I instantly call Shane and Coral, and we agree to meet at the cemetery's gate.

"Amy." Mom watches me like a hawk as I am leaving. "Do you need a ride somewhere?"

"No, thanks, Mom. I'm just going out to enjoy some fresh air."

"If you start feeling tired, or dizzy…"

"I'll come straight back home, in an ambulance."

"Not funny."

"Bye, Mom."

As I leave home, I am blinded by the sunlight. I feel as if the sun and I haven't met for a very long time.

"Hello, girl," says Alex, the neighbor. He is standing outside, watering his plants with a hose. Moka, his dog, sits next to him.

"Hello, Alex."

"Were you sick?"

"Yes… I hit my head."

He nods.

"What's wrong with Moka?" I ask, noticing a large scratch along her back.

"She hurt herself a couple of weeks ago," he says, turning the water off. "She was probably fighting with another dog."

I look at Moka. She opens her mouth, her tongue lolling, as if she is laughing. The scratch on her back doesn't look like something a dog would do.

"You know..." I say. "Two weeks ago someone was chasing me. He wanted to hurt me."

"Yes?"

"And I think a dog pounced on him, and bit him."

"Really?"

"I don't know who or what it was, but it probably saved my life."

"Sounds like you were lucky."

"Alex, do you know what I'm talking about?"

He looks at me with a piercing look and says, "Do I? No. But I told you, some things are better left alone."

"Yes, but maybe Moka..."

"Moka is a good dog," he says. "She does only what she's told."

"Okay. Have a nice day Alex."

"You too, Amy."

The way to the cemetery isn't long, but the heat weighs on me, wearing me down. My steps become slower, heavier, and I begin to regret not asking Mom to give me a ride. I consider calling her. My hand reaches for my phone...

"She no longer wanders at night," a throaty voice suddenly says, making me start. Edgar is smiling at me, standing in the shade of a large tree. Was he there the entire time? How could I have missed him?

"She has stopped running away," he says. "She was really beautiful. And very kind, too."

"She... what? I don't..."

"It's hot, isn't it?" he says.

"Yes," I answer, feeling unsettled. "Who were you talking about? Kimberly? Did you mean that Kimberly–"

"Do you know what's really good?"

"What?" I ask, taking a deep breath.

"Ice cream. How I used to love eating ice cream on a day like this."

"Yes. But, Edgar, who isn't wandering at night?"

"I'm talking about ice cream like they used to make. Not this modern low-fat thing. And definitely not mint-flavored ice cream. I don't even know what that's about."

I realize that he's not about to add anything useful. I say goodbye and begin walking away when his voice makes me halt once more.

"It's silent right now. Dormant. It hardly ever appears, and when it does, no one gets hurt. Maybe a bird, or a small rabbit, nothing more."

"Who?" I ask.

"But it'll change. There is another one, kept in secret. It will find that not all is as it believes, and then... it will emerge."

"What will emerge?"

"The predator." His eyes stare into mine, unblinking. "People are about to die."

I say nothing, simply turn and run away. My breathing is rapid, panicky, my head is bursting in pain, my entire body hurts, but I run, leaving this madman behind me. Eventually the pounding in my skull makes me stop, and I stand, breathing heavily, massaging my forehead.

It's only Edgar. Who knows what he meant? He says all those things, and who could even guess if what he's talking about already happened, or is happening right now, or will maybe happen only decades away? I resume walking towards the cemetery, doing my best to forget this conversation.

Coral and Shane are waiting for me near the gate. Coral hugs me and I hug her back, then take a step backwards and hold her hand in mine.

"You had the stitches removed?"

She nods. "Yes, two days ago."

The scar on her hand still looks nasty, but it seems much better than before. It turned out that she had lost a lot of blood that night, cutting her hand on the broken window.

I consider telling them about my conversation with Edgar, then decide against it. "Do you know where–"

Coral nods. "I came here yesterday. The grave is over there."

She leads Shane and me through the tombstones.

"How are you sleeping?" Shane asks me.

"I sleep like a rock," I answer.

"No whistling?"

"No whistling, no nightmares, no nothing. I sleep all night."

"That's nice."

"It's very nice."

"Here it is," says Coral.

I look at the two tombstones, Patricia White's, and her daughter's, Kimberly White.

I think about Kimberly, trapped helplessly in Tom Ellis's dark basement. Scared, weak, losing all hope. How she nearly got away… but only nearly. Her mother didn't know what happened to Kimberly up till the day she died. She must have hoped that her daughter was still alive. I think about my mom and dad. What would they have done if I'd disappeared like that? If Coral hadn't been there to pull me out the window, if Shane hadn't caught Tom Ellis's attention to help me get away? These thoughts, about my parents, and about those few terrible moments on the floor of the basement, make me tear up.

"I don't even know why I came here," I say hoarsely.

Coral and Shane stay silent.

"I never even knew her," I say. "Only in my dreams… I… I think I want to leave now."

We keep staring at the tombstones for a while.

"Let's go to Shane's," I finally say.

"How about my house?" Coral suggests.

"But Shane's house is closer." I wipe my eyes.

"Yeah, but my Mom made lunch…"

"Fine, fine. What did she make? Soup?"

"Why? Do you want soup?"

"Are you nuts? In this heat?" We leave the cemetery.

"I think she made roast beef and mashed potatoes. You want me to call and ask?"

"I'm sure whatever she made is great," says Shane.

"Yes," I agree. "Even if it's soup."

"Maybe I should call anyway. You know, to let her know I'm bringing friends over."

"Great," says Shane.

"She likes it when I tell her in advance…"

"No problem," I say.

"I'm calling."

I glance backwards and notice someone standing next to the tombstones, her head lowered. A second later she lifts it, and our eyes meet. Patricia? I blink. No. There's no one there. It was just a trick of the light.

"Amy, is everything okay?" asks Shane.

"Yeah," I say. "Everything's great."

CHAPTER THIRTY-EIGHT

I'm sitting by my desk, trying to solve my math homework. I've lost too many school days. Coral is doing her best to help me catch up, but sometimes I feel like a lost cause.

My phone rings. It's Nicole.

"Honey!!!" she screams in my ear.

"Nicole, please try to remember, concussion. I need peace and quiet," I remind her.

"But honey, you really have to hear what happened today…"

Apparently, Trish, from a different class, wore exactly the same outfit that Jennifer Williams wore, and Trish knew very well that Jennifer really loved those pants. She bought them a week ago, so Trish bought exactly the same pair. Jennifer was so pissed! And Trish's ass looked so much better in those pants, so Jennifer swore she'd never wear them again…

"Incredible," I say. "That Trish."

"Honey, how're you feeling?"

"As if I have to study math, and you're bothering me."

"But, honey, I really miss you," she complains. "You promised you'd come over more than two weeks ago, and instead you broke into the house of a murderer, who nearly killed you, and got a concussion."

"Yup."

"You could've simply come over, instead."

"True."

"We would have ordered pizza."

"That sounds good."

"Will you come over this weekend?"

"Sure," I agree."I'd love to."

"And… honey?"

"What?"

"When the hell are you going to update your blog?"

"Bye, Nicole."

"Bye!"

I hang up, and stare out my window. I recall my last conversation with Edgar.

"The predator," I imagine his hoarse voice. "People are about to die."

I shake my head and banish the thought. I look gloomily at my homework. Apparently, x and y are having a mild disagreement. The y-axis is colliding with the function, or is it the x-axis? Is colliding even the right word? Do mathematical variables collide?

I sigh. Only in Narrowdale do math teachers hate students so much.

Only in Narrowdale do math teachers suck students' blood to live forever.

Only in Narrowdale do math teachers turn into bats when there's a full moon.

This isn't working out. The function will have to collide with the y-axis tomorrow. I turn on my laptop and enter my blog's URL.

It's hot today. I get up and turn on the air conditioner. A cold breeze starts blowing around my room. I close my eyes and smile. Then I start to type.

"Hey girls," I write. "Only in Narrowdale are the math teachers blood-sucking vampires."

It's my blog. I'll say whatever I want in it.

Want to Know What Happens Next?

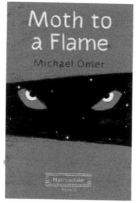

That's great! The sequel, *"Moth to a Flame"* can be purchased
at: **http://www.amazon.com/dp/B00ZR05W56**
If you want to get updates about the next books in the series,
and occasional extra bonuses, subscribe to my newsletter at:
www.strangerealm.com/news
If you liked this book, consider leaving a review at:
http://www.amazon.com/dp/B00S433SWM

If you want to let me know what you thought of the book, feel
free to contact me at: **michael@strangerealm.com**

About the Author

My name is Michael Omer, and I'm a writer, journalist and game designer. I wrote and published my first novel when I was sixteen, and figured I'd keep at it. Since then, I have published two more novels, and wrote… who can even count how many? I'm happily married to a woman who keeps pushing me to write more, and have three kids who insist I should stop writing and come play with them. I also have two dogs.

Let's not mention the fish. I should really do something about the fish.

You can contact me at michael@strangerealm.com

Acknowledgments

This book and I went through a lot together, but we didn't do it alone. Not even close.

First and foremost, I want to thank Liora, my wife. Without her endless support, suggestions and downright instructions, this book would never be here. In fact, it wouldn't be anywhere, except possibly as a half written file somewhere on my hard drive.

Thanks to Alix Reed for editing this book. When the manuscript first reached her hands, it wasn't really a book. It was a collection of words. She did a truly amazing job with it.

Thanks to Eliza Dee for copyediting this document. I didn't know how to punctuate before she went over it. I still don't, but I think I'm learning.

Thanks to Michal Paz-Klap for helping me develop major parts of this book.

Thanks to Rachela Zandbank for being the first one to discover this book.

Thanks to Dorit Debber, my agent, who gave this book all the opportunities it deserved, and even more.

Thanks to Shahar Kober, who created the book's cover for the sheer joy of helping a friend, and for his knowledge about the publishing world which he shared with me.

Thanks to Ziv Sagi, who's room became Amy's room.

Thanks to my sister, Yael Omer, who helped me with insights and thoughts about teenage girls. There are large parts of Amy's character which are based on her.

Thanks to Moshe Malka for helping me format Amy's blog.

Thanks to my parents and my brother Noam for their support and advice.

Thanks to Dori Dayan, for all his advice and practical help. Without him, this book would have never gotten here.
Thanks to Sophie Miller for providing me with valuable information regarding the school system in the US.
Thanks to Shir Hammer, Benny Cohen, Nikki Norris, Darren Lustman, Brad Smith, Josh Flint and Christine Mancuso for reading this manuscript in different stages and helping me polish it.

Made in the USA
Middletown, DE
15 July 2019